Tansy turned round.

'Well, hi there,' sa   meet again.'

Tansy's heart soared.

PJ was Phil Douglas. The TV guy. He was Beth's new man and he was here. In her house.

'Hi!' she said, giving him what she hoped was a winning smile. 'Great to see you again!'

If I play this one right, thought Tansy, I can't lose.

What a Week

to Make it Big

Rosie Rushton

PUFFIN BOOKS

For Ellen, Ursula, the two Claires,
Alex, Matthew, Nick, and the two Sarahs –
a constant source of inspiration!

PUFFIN BOOKS

Published by the Penguin Group
Penguin Books Ltd, 27 Wrights Lane, London W8 5TZ, England
Penguin Putnam Inc., 375 Hudson Street, New York, New York 10014, USA
Penguin Books Australia Ltd, Ringwood, Victoria, Australia
Penguin Books Canada Ltd, 10 Alcorn Avenue, Toronto, Ontario, Canada M4V 3B2
Penguin Books (NZ) Ltd, 182–190 Wairau Road, Auckland 10, New Zealand

Penguin Books Ltd, Registered Offices: Harmondsworth, Middlesex, England

First published 1998
1 3 5 7 9 10 8 6 4 2

Set in Monotype Baskerville
Typeset by Rowland Phototypesetting Limited,
Bury St Edmunds, Suffolk

Made and printed in England by Clays Ltd, St Ives plc

British Library Cataloguing in Publication Data
A CIP catalogue record for this book is
available from the British Library

ISBN 0–140–38761–7

MONDAY

A Problem Shared
Heaven magazine's
Dee Davies talks it over

Dear Dee,
My father is ruining my life. He criticizes my clothes, moans that I wear too much make-up and won't let me stay out late like all my friends. He is really off with my mates too. My mum travels away on business a lot and when I tell her what he's like she just says that I'm lucky he cares. Please tell me how to make him see I have to get a life.
Sarah Lovell (age 14)

Tansy Meadows sighed, tossed her magazine on to the floor and kicked off her duvet. That kid didn't know she was born – at least she had a father to argue with. Tansy wouldn't have minded dragging a dad into the twentieth century had she been lucky enough to have one. All her friends had fathers some-where or other – even Jade Williams had a dead one – but Tansy's

1

problem wasn't how her paternal parent behaved. Her dilemma was that she hadn't a clue who he was.

Her mother, Clarity, who had once been a New Age Traveller and was very good at yoga and caring for small forests and not much good at noting the parentage of her child, assured Tansy that the choice was limited to two: Jordan, who had spent a whole summer painting pebbles in a dilapidated bus parked outside Glastonbury, or Pongo, an American university student from Illinois, who was a great source of comfort to the grief-stricken Clarity when Jordan decided to abandon the pebbles and set off for the Faeroe Islands with a flaxen-haired girl called October.

Tansy hoped it was Pongo – after all, with a university degree, he could by now be rich and famous, with a home in Florida and holidays in the Bahamas. You don't, she thought, get wealthy drawing on stones. Money meant a great deal to Tansy, largely because to date she had not seen as much of it as she would have liked. Her mother, who earned a sort of living from gardening, said that job satisfaction and communing with nature meant more than large pay cheques. Personally, Tansy couldn't understand how anyone would prefer talking to a cauliflower when they could be engaged in some serious shopping.

The older she got, the more Tansy daydreamed about finding her father. Back in primary school, when she had had to write stories about 'Me and

My Family', she would invent a father who had fair hair just like her and who gave her piggybacks and took her to the zoo. As she got older, she gave this father a job on an oil rig, to account for his non-appearance at school sports day or Christmas concerts. Of course in the end, she had to give up pretending and just told people that her dad had left when she was a baby. But that didn't stop her imagining that one day she would find him.

Tansy knew that this was pretty unlikely. Jordan must have got tired of the Faeroe Islands and could be anywhere in the world, and all she knew about Pongo Price was that he had been a student in 1984, sang country and western songs and liked English fish and chips. She didn't even know the name of the town he came from. Her mother said he was fun and spunky and that they had met on the top of Glastonbury Tor while he was on a walking tour of Somerset, trying to find his ancestral home. Tansy had pestered her mother continuously to tell her more, but Clarity said there was no more to tell. Pongo had spent a couple of months with the travellers, during which time Clarity, still seething with anger at the departed Jordan, had fallen for him in a fairly major kind of way. And then, one morning, he was gone.

'But he must have left an address or something,' Tansy would insist. 'You don't have a passionate fling with someone and just leave it at that.'

3

'Well, we did!' her mother would reply shortly. 'Now just forget it, please.'

But Tansy never did forget it.

She wanted a father – and one with an ancestral home sounded hugely promising.

Because the other thing that Tansy was adamant about was that she was going to be Somebody. Anybody. As long as it meant she could live in a house with her own TV and video and fitted carpets and a jacuzzi and never have to hear the phrase 'We can't afford it' again. She wanted to be recognized when she walked down the street and to hear people whisper, 'That's Tansy Meadows – you know, she's the famous . . .'

Only at this point Tansy got a bit stuck. Some days it was 'famous film star', on others it was 'chat-show host' and once in a while, when she had been chosen for the debating team, it turned into 'the well-known politician'. Whatever it turned out to be, Tansy had made one vow. She would never, ever be ordinary.

In view of this ambition, it was, she thought ruefully as she pulled her school sweater over her head and brushed her sandy-coloured flyaway hair, pretty unfair that she was hampered by an excessively ordinary body. She had eyes the colour of snail shells, tiny features and a skinny frame which made her very fast over hurdles and, in her opinion, utterly unacceptable in clingy Lycra. Her mother, who was well built with a mass of auburn

4

hair and the sort of placid disposition that simply couldn't get agitated about things like zits and broken fingernails, told her that she was worrying unnecessarily. But then, thought Tansy, what would you expect of a woman whose idea of make-up was to slap some moisturiser on her cheeks before facing the elements and who on special occasions wore bright-blue eyeshadow which appeared to have been layered on with one of her gardening trowels. Clarity wore floaty Indian cotton dresses when she was at home and cord dungarees while she was working and said things like, 'Your body is simply a dwelling place for your soul.' To which Tansy was prone to reply that her soul would feel a lot happier if its dwelling place could be clothed in a Kookaï cardigan and a charcoal suede miniskirt.

'Tansy! It's getting late – breakfast's on the table!' Her mother's voice carried up the stairs.

'Just a minute!' Tansy puckered her lips and applied a generous amount of Peach Passion lip-gloss. Miss Partridge would probably tell her to wipe it off, but hopefully not until she had thrown a few alluring smiles in the direction of the gorgeous Todd Butler.

She cluttered down the uncarpeted staircase and went through to the kitchen. As she opened the door, an overpowering smell of spices assailed her nostrils.

'Yuk!' she gasped. 'What on earth . . .?'

'Now, darling, don't do your usual thing,'

pleaded her mother, poking at the frying pan determinedly. 'Just try these before you say anything.'

She put a plate of what appeared to be burnt potato cakes in front of Tansy, who prodded them suspiciously with a fork. Despite having given up the travelling lifestyle when Tansy was a baby, her mother was still in what could only be called the experimental stage of home cooking.

'They're awfully good, darling,' enthused her mother, brushing a strand of damp hair from her face. 'Spiced lentil cakes.'

Tansy put down her fork and turned to face her mother.

'Mum,' she said, in the gentle tone one employs when addressing those of limited brain power, 'most people have things like cereal and toast for breakfast. Some even go as far as doing something interesting with a sausage. No one in their right mind eats lentils, spiced or otherwise.'

Clarity sighed.

'Oh, darling, you really are so limited in your view of food. Did you know that in countries where they eat a lot of pulses, they have far fewer cases of heart disease?'

'And a lot more cases of stomach cramp, I shouldn't wonder,' said Tansy. 'Thanks but no thanks.'

Clarity sighed again.

'Laurence says that today's teenagers eat far too

much junk food and it is up to parents to re-educate their palates,' she said.

That, thought Tansy with a sinking heart, explained it. Laurence was the latest in a collection of boyfriends that her mother had acquired over the years and simply served as further proof that, when it came to men, her mother shouldn't be allowed out on her own. Some of the others had been pretty dire but Laurence was something else. He had the haircut from hell, the kind of smarmy smile that made you want to throw up and an irritating habit of being jolly all the time. He was a librarian with the Schools Library Service and thought that made him a world authority on everything. What was majorly embarrassing was the way he kept turning up at school with boxes of books and insisting on chatting to Tansy whenever he saw her – which meant she had to acknowledge that she knew him. Worst of all, he kept telling Tansy how he wanted them to be 'best buddies'. Having a mother with rotten taste in men was bad enough, but how she had the nerve to fall for someone who talked like a character in a bad movie was beyond belief.

Despite all Laurence's shortcomings, Tansy hadn't been too worried at first. Clarity normally kept her relationships on a pretty low-key footing and waved a firm goodbye if things got too involved, but time was marching on in Laurence's case. Clarity had gone all dewy-eyed and glowy and had started wearing tangerine lipstick, which made her

look like a rather surprised hen. Tansy really felt
that the time was coming when she would have to
intervene.

'That guy is so weird,' muttered Tansy, pushing
her plate away and going to the fridge. 'Surely you
can do better than him?'

Clarity turned pink and dropped her eyes.

'He's a dear man with very sound values,' she
insisted. 'And he's extremely knowledgeable.'

'He's a patronizing git!' muttered Tansy, ripping
the top off a hazelnut yoghurt. 'He talks to you as if
you've got half a brain.'

Clarity pulled back her shoulders and bristled.

'He's broadening my horizons,' she said. 'And he
likes to take care of me which makes a nice change.
Anyway, I'd like you to try to get to know him
better.'

She fiddled with a strand of curly hair like a
teenager on a first date.

'I mean, I get the feeling that Larry might be
around for a long time.'

Tansy was so gobsmacked that she dropped her
carton of yoghurt on to the floor.

'You're not . . . I mean, you don't intend to . . .'

Clarity held up her hand.

'I'm not saying anything, it's far too soon,' she
said. 'We shall have to wait and see. He wants to
take me skiing for New Year. He's very special.'

She took a sip of dandelion coffee.

'Special! Mum, he is mega awful!' gasped Tansy,

picking bits of hazelnut off the tiled floor and trying to picture her chunky mother hurtling down a mountainside in a snowsuit. 'You can't be serious. And no way can you go on holiday with him.'

'Why on earth not?' demanded her mother.

'You hardly know the guy,' remonstrated Tansy. You would have thought that by now her mother would have some grasp on morality.

Her mother looked pained.

'So can't I have a life?' she asked. 'Anyway, I think it's written in my path of destiny. Madame Zarborski saw a man with a pile of books in her crystal ball.'

Tansy raised her eyes heavenwards.

'Oh, for heaven's sake, Mum!' she snapped. 'You are so gullible. You've probably told her a zillion times that you're going out with a librarian. Anyway, I thought you said you weren't going to any more clairvoyants after she told you that she saw large sums of money the night before you beat me at Monopoly.'

Clarity said nothing, so Tansy tried again.

'You can do much better than Laurence, Mum,' she said persuasively. 'What do you see in him?'

Clarity screwed up her eyes and smiled dreamily.

'He makes me feel wanted and cherished. And he's sensible and sorts me out. Besides, you've always said you wanted a father, haven't you, darling?'

This, thought Tansy, is seriously dangerous.

'Not just any old father!' she snapped. 'My own father, yes!'

'Oh, darling, let it rest – that's all in the past now.'

'It isn't *in* the past, it *is* my past!' retorted Tansy, her throat tightening in the way it always did when her mum got all dismissive. How dare she expect to fob her off with a nerd in cord flares who had all the charisma of a dying pot plant?

'You just don't care how I feel, do you?' she snapped accusingly.

Clarity shrugged.

'I do care – but after all, what is the point of tormenting yourself over a father you will never meet – someone who doesn't even know you exist? Forget it, darling. What's done is done.'

Tears pricked at the back of Tansy's eyes and she swallowed hard.

'Oh, and that's it, is it? Oh great. Terrific. This is my life we're talking about. But you couldn't care less about who my real dad is, do you? You didn't care who you hung out with then and you don't care now!'

Tansy stopped. She couldn't believe she said that. Her mum stared at her, open-mouthed.

'That's not true,' she said softly and Tansy saw that her eyes were damp. 'But whatever mistakes I made, I can't change the past. The future is what matters now.'

Tansy was about to reply when there was a repeated knocking on the back door. Clarity, relieved to have a diversion, peered through the window.

'Oh, it's Andy, darling!' she chirped. 'How nice!'

Tansy cringed. How come Andy Richards, who had sticking-out ears and crooked front teeth, followed her around like a forlorn puppy, while Todd Butler, who was funny, drop-dead gorgeous and had money to burn, ignored her very existence? Life was excessively unfair.

'Tell him I've left already,' she hissed, jumping up from the table and sidling through to the sitting room.

'But Tansy . . .' began her mother, her hand on the back-door handle.

'Mum!' There was no mistaking Tansy's warning tone. 'Do it!'

Clarity sighed, opened the door, and did as she was told.

Tansy flopped into an armchair and reflected on her life. She knew at thirteen and three-quarters she should really be in love. Or at least very much in like. But the only guy who made her stomach flip and her heart race, like all the magazines said they should, was Todd, who didn't even notice when Tansy deliberately bumped into him. She had got pretty near to it last term with Trig Roscoe, who was American and had the most amazing eyes. But when her best friend, Holly Vine, had had her somewhat disastrous birthday party, Trig had been all over Cleo Greenway and now they were a total item. She tried not to be jealous, because Cleo was a mate, but she did wonder how it was that her timid, anxious and overweight friend could get the only fit guy in Year Nine without even trying.

Her mother finally returned from what appeared to be an unnecessarily long conversation on the doorstep.

'Sweetheart,' she said encouragingly, 'Andy does seem such a nice boy.'

With a track record like yours, thought Tansy, I would do well to avoid any guy you deem suitable. Besides, I want passion and Andy just isn't passion material. Whereas Todd . . .

'So why don't you like him?' her mother persisted. 'I mean, he's —'

'Mum! It's my life, OK. And I hardly think you are qualified to comment on boys.'

Clarity pursed her lips and turned away.

'It's late,' Tansy mumbled. 'I'll see you tonight.'

She stood up and picked up her school bag.

'Anything exciting happening this week?' Clarity asked, in an attempt to put the conversation on a less-risky footing.

Tansy shook her head.

'Exciting?' she snapped. 'At West Green Upper? In your dreams.'

8.30 a.m. Top-secret news

As Tansy turned into Weston Way she saw Holly and Cleo walking ahead of her, deep in conversation. Usually Tansy was pleased to see her friends and to catch up on the news from the weekend, but this morning she had a lump in her throat and didn't feel like talking. She slackened her pace and hoped they wouldn't turn round and spot her.

Perhaps her mum was right, she thought. Perhaps she should just put all ideas about her somewhere-father out of her mind and accept that she would never know who he was. After all, she had managed for nearly fourteen years without knowing. But for some reason which she didn't really understand, not knowing about one half of herself was getting harder, not easier.

She did feel rather guilty for having yelled at her mum. She guessed she must get lonely at times, although in Tansy's opinion, solitary confinement would be preferable to an evening with the dreadful Laurence. But sometimes she wondered whether her mum really understood what it was like to be fatherless. Even though Tansy's granddad had died suddenly three years earlier from a heart attack, he had always been there while Clarity was growing up so she had loads of memories about her own father. She knew that her auburn hair came from his side of the family and that he loved dark chocolate and Westerns and was brilliant at drawing and terrible at remembering where he put things. And most importantly of all, she knew that he loved her.

Clarity had told her often enough how it was Granddad that had stood up for her when she returned home at eighteen, broke and four months pregnant with Tansy. He had understood when she refused to have an abortion and had taken her side when she had told them that she wanted to keep the baby. And he had smoothed everything over when Gran had totally flipped and refused to talk to Clarity for days.

It wasn't even as if Tansy could pump Gran for information, because she had re-married and now lived in Scotland. She sent Tansy presents on her birthday and at Christmas, and they talked on the telephone. But whenever Tansy brought up the subject of fathers, Gran would simply say, 'Best let sleeping dogs lie,' and start telling her all the wonderful things that darling Beth was doing.

Beth! Tansy's mind started racing. Her mother's sister was twenty-two – ten years younger than Clarity – and a real high-flyer. She lived in London, in a tiny flat right on the King's Road and worked as a feature writer for *Savoir Faire* which was the sort of magazine people put on coffee tables because it showed their friends that they had good taste. Beth had a wicked sense of humour and changed her boyfriends as often as Tansy's mum, but at least Beth chose presentable ones with decent cars and the ability to match the right socks to their trousers.

Tansy had never talked to Beth about Pongo or Jordan – after all, Beth had only been eight when Tansy was born and no one would have told her anything but she might have some ideas on how Tansy could get more information. She might even be able to persuade Mum to open up or get Gran to tell her something. It wasn't very likely, but the way Tansy was feeling right now, anything was worth a try. She was tired of being fobbed off with feeble excuses. It was time everyone started treating her like an adult. And Beth was more likely to do that than anyone.

Once she had made that decision she felt better and by the time she caught up with her friends at the bus stop, she was smiling broadly and looking her normal, cheerful self.

'Hi, Tansy – guess what?' Holly Vine was hopping up and down on one leg in excitement, her nutmeg-brown hair flopping over her face.

'You're in love again?' suggested Tansy. She knew that Holly's main aim in life was to get a guy and, generally speaking, when her friend was in high spirits a boy was involved somewhere.

'No, silly – although one of the boys who are going to be moving into the new house behind us is to die for.'

Cleo and Tansy exchanged 'here we go again' glances and grinned.

'No,' continued Holly excitedly, 'it's even better than that! You know *Go For It!* – that TV game show on Saturday mornings?'

Tansy nodded. *GFI!* was one of the coolest shows for teens on cable – everyone watched it, partly

15

because of Ben Bolter, the dishy presenter, and partly because it was so wickedly off the wall and different from any other show on TV.

'Go on,' urged Cleo. 'Tell her.'

'Well,' began Holly, savouring her role as bringer of great tidings. 'They're coming to Dunchester. For Saturday's show! And West Green Upper's going to be one of the schools taking part!'

Tansy's eyes widened in disbelief.

'You're kidding!' she breathed. 'How do you know? No one ever knows.'

What made *GFI!* so different from anything else on TV was its unpredictability. Schools wrote in for a chance to send a team of kids, but it wasn't until the week of the live show that they got to know whether they had been picked.

Go For It! was all about ambition and making dreams come true. It had Go for Cash, Go for Glory and Go for the Top rounds, and if your team got through to the final round, you each got to Go for IT – your own personal dream. The prizes were ace, and the whole thing was brilliant viewing. To take part, thought Tansy, would be the funkiest thing ever.

'Isn't it great?' said Cleo, hitching her rucksack over her shoulder as the school bus came round the corner. 'Who do you reckon will get on the team?'

Me, if I have anything to do with it, thought Tansy, her brain whirring as she imagined being spotted by a talent scout and whisked off to a life of indulgence on a film set in Beverly Hills. This could be my passport to fame.

'But how do you know they're really coming?' she asked Holly again, as the bus pulled up. She couldn't afford to get excited and then discover that Holly had got the wrong end of the stick.

'Miss Partridge let it slip to my dad at one of their stupid dressing-up sessions,' Holly explained.

Holly's father was an historian who wrote intelligent books all week and then behaved in a most unintelligent manner at weekends, dressing up as a Roundhead and fighting mock battles at carnivals and county shows. Elinor Partridge, who for obvious reasons was nicknamed Birdie, taught English to Year Nine and had such a sad life that her idea of excitement was to take part in these re-enactments as a bystander or mother of just-killed son (she was very good at weeping to order).

'She wasn't meant to say anything,' said Holly, 'but you know how dippy she is and, apparently, it sort of came out because she has to take the team to *GFI!* on Saturday and can't be "A Fallen Woman at the Siege of Camber Hill".'

'And your dad actually told you?' queried Tansy as they piled on to the bus. 'It's meant to be top secret until the last minute.'

'My father', sighed Holly, 'is not of the real world. He hadn't even heard of *GFI!* – can you believe it?'

She glanced quickly round the assortment of kids jostling and chattering around them.

'So don't say a word to anyone else,' she urged, dropping her voice to a whisper. 'Birdie would have a fit if she knew Dad had told me.'

'But we can tell Jade, can't we?' asked Cleo anxiously. 'I mean, if we three know, it's not fair to leave her out, is it?'

Cleo was a firm believer in fair play and keeping everyone happy all the time.

'I don't know,' said Holly hesitantly.

'She won't tell anyone,' urged Cleo, grabbing the handrail as the bus lurched round a corner. 'It might help cheer her up.'

Jade Williams had joined their set last term when she had come to Dunchester to live with her aunt, who already had three kids of her own. Jade's mum and dad had been killed in a car accident and even though she was trying hard to get over it, she had spells when she was really down in the dumps. Cleo thought it must be the most awful thing in the world to suddenly find yourself an orphan. She missed her dad like crazy now he lived with his new girlfriend, Fleur, but at least she got to see him from time to time, and she still had her mum. And, of course, her two sisters, although whether Portia and Lettie qualified as things to be thankful for was somewhat debatable. Even with all the rows between her mum and stepdad, Roy, and her mum and Portia, and Lettie and Portia, and practically every other combination you could think of, Cleo reckoned she was a lot luckier than Jade, who must feel really alone.

Holly chewed her lip and looked thoughtful.

'Come on,' urged Cleo. 'You're not still miffed with her, are you?'

Actually, yes, thought Holly. After all, it was me that stood by Jade when she first came to West Green Upper, and then she actually chose my birthday party to snog the guy I fancy. Scott Hamill could still make Holly's toes curl with desire, and the fact that he and Jade had been a major item since the party didn't help Holly to feel kindly disposed towards her.

But she was basically a pretty fair person and knew deep down that it wasn't actually Jade's fault that Scott fancied her more than Holly. Rotten, tragic, heartbreaking and very short-sighted on Scott's part – but not Jade's fault.

'OK,' she said at last, 'but absolutely and positively no one else. Cross your heart?'

'And hope to die,' asserted Cleo.

'Promise,' echoed Tansy, whose mind was working overtime. She had to get on this show. She simply had to.

'How do you think they choose people?' she asked Holly, trying to sound as if it didn't matter to her in the slightest.

'I'm not sure,' admitted Holly. 'But I reckon this is a good week to suck up to the teachers.'

'I read in a magazine that they send people from the show into schools,' said Cleo. 'Only you don't know they are from *GFI!* – they pretend to be

19

someone else.'

'So really', said Tansy, thinking fast, 'we have to be mega nice to the teachers and chat up every stranger we see in school.'

Holly nodded.

'And remember,' she urged, 'they are bound to ask you what your ambition is – that's the whole point of the programme. So we need to think up some pretty mind-blowing ideas that they've never done before.'

'What if you don't have an ambition?' asked Cleo, who currently found that getting through each day with a family like hers was enough to be coping with, never mind thinking years ahead.

'Then you wouldn't get on, would you?' said Tansy in exasperation. 'The idea is that you don't get days and days to think up something wacky, just to get on TV – it has to be what you really want and know something about.'

Holly grinned.

'Of course, we've got a headstart. We know they're coming. I'd die to get on that show.'

Cleo pulled a face.

'I don't somehow think pulling a dozen guys in five days is allowed as an ambition,' she teased. 'Anyway, none of us know what we want to do for sure.'

Speak for yourself, thought Tansy. She had so many ambitions, the problem would be choosing one. Not that even *GFI!* could grant her dearest

wish. Finding fathers wasn't part of the programme's schedule. But getting on TV would mean
being noticed and she was determined that
somehow she was going to get picked. No matter
what it took.

9.00 a.m. During registration

Holly, Cleo and Tansy looked for Jade, eager to tell
her the secret. She was nowhere to be seen.

'Maybe she's missed the bus,' said Cleo.

'Or perhaps she's ill,' suggested Tansy. 'We could
phone in the lunch hour and find out.'

'And tell her about *Go For* –' began Cleo and
stopped when the cap of Holly's trouser boot
addressed her left ankle.

'I told you not to say a word,' said Holly. 'Your
voice can be heard right across the room.'

Cleo looked suitably apologetic. As the school's
star soprano, she was used to being told to project
her voice, which was useful in school plays and
when subduing her little sister, Lettie, but not a
great advantage in the keeping of secrets.

'Do you want to get chosen for you-know-what?'
Tansy asked Cleo. She had been pondering on just
how awful it would be if one of them got chosen and
not the others. Particularly if she was one of the
others.

Cleo shook her head.

'All those people watching me make an idiot of
myself? No, thank you. What about you, Holly?'

Holly nodded eagerly.

'You bet,' she said. 'Just think of all the guys you'd get to meet from the other teams.'

'Is *every* decision you make governed by boys?' sighed Cleo in mock desperation.

'Yes,' said Holly happily, and began day-dreaming about the sexy brothers who would soon be her over-the-fence neighbours.

11.15 a.m. Cleo makes plans

It was boys – or rather one particular boy – that occupied Cleo's own thoughts in Geography. Thinking about Trig Roscoe was a lot more gripping than considering oxbow lakes. Cleo had never expected to get a boyfriend; she had always thought that because she was fat, useless at sport and blushed easily, she would always be the one without a guy. But at Holly's fourteenth birthday party, Trig Roscoe, who was American and had hair the colour of a crème brûlée, had actually asked her out. Her! Not Tansy, who was small and lively and always remembered the punchlines to jokes; not Holly, who was tall and willowy and never worried; but her. Dumpy, boring Cleo. Even more surprisingly, Cleo had said yes. Since she had spent the previous week thinking that Trig was an arrogant poser with attitude, this was quite a turnaround. But she had discovered that all Trig's apparent confidence and boasting about girlfriends back in Illinois was just a ploy to hide his worries

22

about his body. He had a huge scarlet birthmark which ran from his neck to his waist and even though he was easily the best-looking guy in Year Nine, he seemed to think that no girl would give him a second look once they knew.

In the few weeks since they had got together, Cleo had discovered that Trig's life was pretty tough even though all the kids at school reckoned that dashing off round the world for a year at a time was the height of glam living. Trig's dad was an ex-Marine who worked in IT and earned wads of money. He was in England for a year setting up a complicated computer system for an American bank and they lived in a big rented house in Dulverton Road. Trig's elder brother, Pierce, was on a sports scholarship at an American university and Jodie, his seventeen-year-old sister, had decided to stay in Chicago because she was representing Illinois in the Junior Sportathon.

'I'm hoping my dad will get to like me better, now there's only me at home,' Trig had told Cleo the previous Monday as they dawdled home from school.

'What do you mean?' Cleo had asked in surprise. 'Of course he likes you.'

'Not really,' Trig had muttered. 'Not as much as Pierce and Jodie anyway. They are really into athletics and sport and all that stuff – Pierce is six-foot-four and he plays American football and baseball and runs for his uni. I'm useless at all

23

that stuff – my dad says I'm a total waste of space.'

Cleo had gasped. That was awful – the sort of thing you expect bullies in the playground to yell at you, not your own father.

'I expect he was just joking,' Cleo had assured him, secretly thinking that it was a pretty poor kind of joke.

Trig shrugged.

'Maybe,' he had said. 'But like I told you at Holly's party, Dad's really into body-building and action stuff. He keeps on at me to get a life and stop being a nerd.'

'You're not a nerd! You're clever and funny and you like a laugh. And you know so much about history.'

Trig had sighed.

'Oh yeah – great, isn't it? I mean, "I like history" doesn't sound quite as cool as "I scored a home run" or "I'm captain of the hockey squad", does it?' He had pulled off his Chicago B's baseball cap and twiddled it round in his fingers.

'Dad says real guys don't bury themselves in the past but go out and create the future. That's his favourite line.'

Cleo liked Mr Roscoe less the more she heard about him.

Trig had shrugged.

'I guess that until I do something earth-shatteringly wonderful, Dad will still just keep on at me. He's a great one for fame and recognition. And there's not much chance of me getting either of those in Dunchester, is there?'

When he had said that, Cleo had felt quite sorry for him. But now, sitting in Beetle's boring geography lesson, the seed of an idea crept into her mind.

If Trig could get on to *GFI!*, he could show his dad that he was up there with the cool guys. And if he did well, his dad would be really proud of him which would do Trig's confidence the power of good.

And of course, if Trig took part in *GFI!*, Cleo could go along to cheer from the audience. And give him a congratulatory kiss at the end. Which wouldn't exactly be bad for Cleo either.

The whole thing was luck, of course. But if only she could find out who was doing the choosing, there might be a way to give luck a bit of a helping hand.

11.45 a.m.
Bonjour, mes enfants!
Tansy chewed the end of her rollerball and re-read her first paragraph with some satisfaction.

Monday – in French

Hi, Beth!
I am writing to you because I need your help to sort out something really important and I reckon you are the only person around who is going to take me seriously and not treat me like some dippy kid.

Beth was bound to sit up and take notice after an opening like that.

'Tansy Meadows! What are you doing?' Mrs Chapman barked across the classroom.

Tansy slipped the letter underneath *Allez en France, mes enfants!* and smiled winningly.

'Nothing, Mrs Chapman,' she lied.

'Well, instead of concentrating all your undoubted talents on nothing, perhaps you could address yourself to writing three paragraphs on the subject of *Ma Famille en Vacances* which means . . .?'

Mrs Chapman waited with that air of hopeful expectation that teachers adopt when school inspectors are due any day.

'My family on holiday,' said Tansy with a sigh.

Momentarily satisfied, Mrs Chapman turned her attention to Ursula Newley's inability to grasp the past tense of *avoir*. Tansy slipped her letter from underneath the book and thought hard. The next bit had to be just right.

Lately I can't stop thinking about my dad — whoever he might be. Mum gets all upset when I mention the subject and you know how Gran just won't talk about it at all. So I was wondering whether you knew anything. I know you were only little when it all happened but if you knew how I could find out a bit more about him — them — it would be wonderful. Mum says it was either a guy called Jordan Walters who went off to the Faeroe

Islands or else a student called Pongo Price from America. I suppose I should have asked Grandad while he was still alive, but when I was younger it didn't seem so important. Now it does. Please tell me anything you know, however small. And please reply really, really soon.

Love, Tansy xxxxx

That sounded about right, thought Tansy with satisfaction. She stuffed the letter into an envelope and rammed it into her rucksack. She could post it on the way home. She felt a little shiver of excitement ripple through her body. Within a few days, she could be on the way to finding a father, and even, if luck was on her side, being discovered by a TV producer as the next Zoë Ball.

I do believe, she thought as the bell rang for lunch break, that my life might actually start to get exciting.

12.45 p.m. Making enquiries

At lunchtime the three girls clustered around the payphone in the locker room and dialled Jade's number.

'Hi, is that Paula? I mean, Mrs . . .' Holly paused. She knew Paula didn't have the same surname as Jade, but she couldn't remember what it was.

'Oh, sorry, Mrs Webb. Yes, well, this is Holly Vine. I was just wondering if Jade is OK?'

The others could hear a gabbling voice at the other end and saw Holly frown.

'Jade – is she OK? I mean, when we realized she wasn't at school, we just wondered whether she . . . oh, I see.' She clamped her hand over the mouthpiece.

'Paula says of course she's at school,' she hissed to her friends. 'You don't think she's bumming off, do you? What shall I say?'

Holly jigged up and down looking worried and Tansy snatched the phone from her hand.

'Hi, Mrs Webb, this is Tansy Meadows,' she chirped. 'Don't worry, it's my fault. One of the guys said Jade was off sick, and I thought he meant your Jade, but he meant Jade Connolley. Jade's probably tied up . . . doing library duty or something. Bye!'

She slammed the receiver on to the cradle and turned to Holly and Cleo.

'Did that sound even vaguely like a true story?' she asked.

She noted their expressions.

'No, I didn't think it did.'

'Do you think we've landed her in it with Paula?' asked Cleo anxiously as they headed towards the cafeteria. 'And if she's not at home, where is she? Shouldn't we tell someone?'

'We can't really,' said Tansy with a frown. 'If we do, she'll be in trouble big time and there's probably a perfectly simple explanation.'

'We could ask Scott,' suggested Cleo who was

always the one with the sensible ideas. 'He's bound to know – they're hardly ever apart these days.'

Holly felt a stab of jealousy hit her in the chest. She had tried and tried to forget Scott Hamill but she still thought that he was the cutest guy in their year and having one of her closest friends hanging out with him didn't help the forgetting process one bit.

'He's over there,' said Cleo, pointing across the crowded cafeteria to a table in the far corner. 'Let's sound him out.'

They pushed through a crowd of Year Sevens who were being even more infantile than usual and moved towards Scott's table. As they passed the drinks machine, Andy Richards appeared from nowhere and nudged Tansy's arm.

'Hi, Tansy,' he said, his cheeks turning bright pink. 'Are you coming to computer club?'

Tansy glared at him.

'Are you?' she asked.

Andy nodded eagerly.

'Then no,' she said, turning away.

'That', said Cleo, 'was not very nice.'

Tansy shrugged.

'He'll never get the message unless I spell it out,' she said. 'Why can't he find someone else to drool over?'

'Because he fancies you, of course,' grinned Cleo. 'He's as crazy about you as Scott is about Jade. I think he's kind of cute. Don't you like being adored?'

Not, thought Tansy, unless it's Todd doing the adoring. And right now there seems little chance of that.

When they reached Scott's table, they saw that Ursula and Nick were with him, and the three were deep in conversation.

'Hi, Scott!' interrupted Tansy, who was never one to observe the niceties of social etiquette. 'Do you know where Jade is?'

Scott looked up.

'No,' he said shortly.

'She's not in school,' added Cleo.

'So?' said Scott, dipping a chip into some tomato sauce. 'Maybe she's ill.'

It occurred to Holly that he didn't seem particularly concerned. Maybe he was falling out of love with Jade already. She knew that shouldn't please her, but it did. A lot.

'She's not ill,' continued Cleo. 'We phoned her house, and her aunt thinks she's in school but she's not.'

For a moment Scott looked concerned.

'And we thought, what with you two being such lovebirds –' began Tansy.

'Get lost!' snapped Scott.

'Pardon?' said Tansy. She had just spotted Todd Butler moving towards them and was trying to look as if she didn't know he was there, while still making sure he noticed her.

'Just leave it out, will you?' Scott interjected.

'You can't fool me – Jade's put you up to this. Well, I'm not that dumb. If she wants to talk to me, she can come and do it face to face. Not', he added, stabbing a fish finger with unnecessary force, 'that I care one way or the other.'

Cleo and Holly stared at him, for once in their lives lost for words. Tansy was too busy smiling extravagantly at the approaching Todd to notice just how angry Scott was looking.

Cleo was the first to recover.

'Hey, hang on a minute!' she retorted. 'I haven't a clue what's going on with you two but this isn't some stupid game. It's the truth. We don't know where Jade is.'

Scott said nothing but lowered his eyes. Tansy was busy pursing her lips in what she hoped was a provocative manner and willing Todd to stop at their table.

'Does it occur to you that Jade could be in some kind of trouble? Anything might have happened to her,' said Cleo sternly. 'That's why I can't help thinking we should tell someone.'

'She's probably just skiving off school,' suggested Ursula. 'It's no big deal.'

'It is with Jade,' asserted Holly. 'She's not the skiving off sort.'

'Yes, well I thought I knew Jade and, boy, was I wrong!' snapped Scott, and Cleo noticed that he was clenching his fists.

31

Tansy sighed. Todd had walked straight past her. He hadn't even noticed her existence.

She turned reluctantly back to the conversation.

'Have you two had a row?' she asked.

'We've split up,' said Scott.

Oh goody, thought Holly. And then felt very guilty for being so delighted.

'That's awful,' said Cleo, thinking that the last thing Jade needed right now was a broken relationship on top of everything else.

'What happened?' asked Tansy. 'You two were such an item.'

'Well, we're not now,' said Scott. 'Just forget it, will you? It's no big deal.'

And with that, he pushed back his chair and stomped off towards the door.

The girls looked at one another.

'What was all that about?' Cleo asked Ursula.

'Scott says that Jade's being really off with him,' replied Ursula, stuffing chips into her mouth. 'He says she's stuck up – apparently she won't go round to his house because she doesn't think his family is good enough.'

Scott came from a big and boisterous family and Holly remembered that there always seemed to be one or more of his mum's Italian relatives staying over. When she was going out with Scott, she never managed to sort out all the different cousins and uncles that kept appearing for tea and talking nineteen to the dozen, switching from fluent Italian to accented English and back again at the speed of light.

'That's ridiculous!' Tansy burst out. 'Jade's nothing like that – he must be crazy!'

Ursula shrugged.

'I'm only saying what he told us,' she said. 'Maybe you should ask her what's going on.'

'We will,' agreed Holly.

'When we find her,' added Cleo.

3.00 p.m. In Beckets Park

Jade sat huddled on a bench in Beckets Park. She couldn't believe she was doing this. She had skived off school for a whole day. She had never, ever done that before and she didn't even care. Or at least, she was trying to convince herself that she didn't care. She knew that if she got found out, she'd be in big trouble but that was tough. Nothing mattered any more. Nothing at all.

She stood up, shoved her hands in her pockets and began wandering down the path towards the kids' playground. Mums were pulling children off the slide and bundling them into pushchairs, ready to fetch their older children from school. Further along, a dad was playing frisbee with a small boy, while an elderly lady nursed a squealing baby. Everywhere she looked, the world was full of families. Proper families. Like she would never have again.

Just for a bit over the past month, she had begun

to think that maybe life would get back to normal one day. She would never forget her parents, never stop missing them for one single second, but when she and Scott had started going out, she had begun to feel that maybe there was someone in the world to whom she would be special. It wasn't that Paula, her mum's sister, or David, Paula's husband, were horrid or anything; they did all they could to make her happy. But they had kids of their own and a whole life before Jade came to live with them, and she felt like an intruder, a sort of spectator watching other people's lives but never being part of them. She knew Allegra, her fourteen-year-old cousin, who went to stage school and had a whole host of really trendy friends, resented Jade's presence. Josh, who was sixteen, simply ignored her. Only Nell, who was seven and pretty timid, seemed to be pleased to have her around. Jade spent a lot of time reading to Nell and playing with her, which caused Allegra to say that she was at last finding someone of her own emotional level. Allegra could win the Olympic gold for cattiness.

Jade kicked at a patch of gravel and sighed. When she and Scott had got together, it had been such a relief to have someone to talk to about anything, someone who didn't seem to mind her chatting about the past. Paula hated it when Jade mentioned her parents but Scott asked her questions and laughed at her stories and made her feel that things might just be getting better.

And then it had all gone horribly wrong. She wished she could turn the clock back, have Saturday all over again. Then she would never have said yes when he asked her back to his house for tea, never have faced that enormous family, never have made such a mess of everything.

She stopped and brushed the tears away from her eyes. She wouldn't think about it. It was over. Scott hated her. He had every right to hate her. She was horrible. No one would ever love her again. She knew that now.

She began wondering how she could avoid school tomorrow.

4 p.m. Muddy and miffed

Clarity Meadows loaded her garden tools into the back of the van and brushed the mud off her dungarees. Usually she found her job as a gardener a real delight, but today, while she was raking up leaves and pruning roses, she had been worrying about Tansy. And wondering whether the past would ever lie down and go to sleep.

She knew it was hard on her daughter, not knowing who her father was. Maybe, she thought as she climbed into the driving seat and slammed the door shut, I did it all wrong. Maybe I should have told her everything when she was small. But how could I? I only did what I thought was right and now she thinks I don't care.

If she had married when Tansy was little, her

35

daughter might not have this desperate need to find her real father. But the right guy never came along. I haven't have a lot of luck with men, she thought as she adjusted the driving mirror and turned the ignition key. Until now. Until Laurence. I think this time things might just work out.

Clarity knew Tansy wasn't very keen on Laurence. But he was kind and generous and most important of all, he took charge of her. It had been great to be wild and independent when she was younger but now she was in her thirties, the novelty was wearing off and having someone to remind her about things like tax returns and taking cod liver oil for her knees was very comforting. It was a shame that Laurence worked so hard as it meant she didn't see him much during the week – and she was beginning to think it would be rather nice if he was around a lot more. It was a long time since Clarity had had someone there for her. And she rather liked it. But she wanted Tansy to be happy too.

It wasn't even as if she could talk it over with any of the other mums. To do so would mean admitting what a mess she had made of things. Angela Vine, Holly's mum, was really nice but Clarity was sure that people like her, who did good works and sat on committees, would think she was a total failure. So would Cleo's mum, who was an actress and who had been in TV adverts and even had a small part in a film with Andie MacDowell. She couldn't talk to her mother, because she was of the mind that

Clarity had made her own bed and should learn to lie in it, which was probably true but not enormously helpful, and Dad, who had understood, was dead. And Beth – well, she still thought of Beth as her baby sister, despite her high-powered job and frenetic social whirl.

Clarity felt very alone. Being a single mum had been hard enough when Tansy was a baby; but that was a doddle compared to knowing what to do now.

Anyway, she told herself firmly, it's probably just a phase Tansy is going through. After all, she thought, teenagers do go through phases, don't they? I did – I was headstrong and ran away and did all sorts of crazy things and I'm perfectly normal now, whatever my daughter says. That's what it will be – just a passing phase.

She kept telling herself that all the way home. But when she pulled up outside the cottage, she still hadn't managed to convince herself.

4.15 p.m. Anxious auntie

Paula Webb had been thinking about that phone call all afternoon. There was something odd about it. First Holly asking how Jade was and then Tansy coming on the line and saying that it was all a mistake and it was another Jade who was ill. It couldn't be that Jade really hadn't turned up at school, could it? Well, of course it couldn't. Jade was such a quiet little mouse, not like her mum Liz, Paula's sister. Paula remembered when she was twelve and Liz was ten, they had gone . . . Stop it. Don't remember. Lizzie's gone. Oh, Lizzie.

Paula shook herself and switched on the kettle. She did so want to get things right with Jade. Of course she worried about her own three, but Jade was Lizzie's daughter and it seemed even more important that she should do everything perfectly for her.

She had thought of telephoning the school, just to check that Jade was there, but then decided against it. After all, the girls must have found Jade or they would have phoned again. And she didn't want to be seen as a worrier.

She looked at the kitchen clock. Normally she would have been at work all day but Nell had tonsillitis and she had brought some work home so that she could be with her. 4.35 p.m. Jade would be in soon and she'd ask her outright. Jade would always tell the truth. She was that sort of child.

4.25 p.m. Thoughts horticultural

Holly's mother stood at the kitchen sink, staring out at the mess that was their back garden. Once it had been beautiful with a long sweeping lawn, lots of fruit trees and a big vegetable garden. But because her husband refused to leave their rambling old house, despite its rattling windows and clanking radiators, and because the bank were not exactly delighted at the size of the Vines' overdraft, they had been forced to sell most of the garden to a builder. He had built two new houses whose curtainless windows glared unsympathetically at Angela Vine as she washed dishes.

'What we really need, Naseby,' she informed the cat who was sitting on the draining board licking a used teabag, 'is a gardener. But gardeners cost money and we don't have any to spare.'

Unless, she thought, I ask Tansy's mum. She might not charge as much as these big landscaping firms. And she's young enough to cope with digging which is more than I am.

Angela was beginning to feel every one of her fifty-four years. She adored Holly but having a child years after you thought your family was complete did come as a bit of a shock and sometimes she thought that she'd made a mess of motherhood third time round. Clarity Meadows was only in her early thirties and, if that delightful Tansy was anything to go by, the perfect parent, despite doing it all single-handed.

There would be no harm in just asking her what it would cost to make a patio and a lawn and maybe a little rockery. With a small fountain, perhaps. They could have a coffee and a chat. She might pick up a few tips on motherhood as well as climbing roses.

Angela began hunting for the telephone directory.

8 p.m. On line for a good idea

Tansy had sat for what seemed like an eternity at the supper table, enduring not only her mother's unique version of fish pie but Laurence's patronizing lecture about how she really should read something more illuminating than *Sugar* magazine.

'I am what I am today because of reading,' he told her.

'Now there's a good reason never to pick up a book again,' remarked Tansy through gritted teeth.

She was spared her mother's irritated riposte by the ringing of the telephone.

'I'll get it,' she cried and fled.

'Dunchester five-seven-seven-zero-seven-eight,' she began.

'Hi, Tansy? It's me, Holly. Listen, I've been thinking about this *Go For It!* thing. You do want to get on it, don't you?'

'Of course I do,' said Tansy, shutting the door in an attempt to blot out Laurence's droning voice. 'Trouble is they could pick anyone.'

'I know,' agreed Holly. 'But at least we know they're coming. What we need are some really unusual ideas to have as our *Go For It!* dream. That's why I'm phoning – what if I say I want to be the nation's youngest newsreader?'

'Do you?' asked Tansy.

'Not especially,' admitted Holly. 'But no one's done that before. What about you?'

'I haven't thought yet,' said Tansy. But the seed of an idea suddenly began sprouting in her mind. I wonder, she thought. I just wonder.

8.30 p.m. Lies down the line

Jade rushed to the telephone and grabbed it on the second ring. After ten minutes of being questioned she had managed to get Paula to believe that she had been at school all day, and one wrong word from any of her friends would really blow it.

'Dunchester eight-double-one-one-two-three,' she gabbled. 'Oh, hi, Cleo – how's it going?'

'Are you OK? Where were you? We rang and Paula said –'

'Did you really?' Jade tried desperately to make it sound as if she was having a perfectly normal conversation. 'And what did he say?'

Cleo paused.

'Someone's listening?'

'Sure,' said Jade, as Paula brushed past her on the way to the kitchen.

'You did bunk off, didn't you?' she said. 'Jade, why? What's happening? And what's with you and Scott?'

Jade's heart sank. He'd told them. She hadn't thought he would do that. Not yet. What had he said?

'What do you mean?' she said, playing for time.

'He said you'd split up,' said Cleo, gently.

Jade's eyes filled with tears. So he really had

41

meant it. And he was telling everyone. She had hoped that he might just change his mind. It was all her fault.

'Jade? Are you still there? Are you OK?'

Jade swallowed and took a deep breath.

'Yes, fine.'

Cleo realized that Jade was far from fine and decided that this was not the time to tell her just what Scott had said about her. Not over the phone.

'Anyway,' she said, adopting a bright and cheerful tone of voice. 'Brilliant news.' And she launched into the story of *GFI!*

Jade listened as Cleo told her about the researchers coming, and made her promise not to say a word. She said yes and no in all the right places and agreed half-heartedly that it would be great if one of their friends were chosen.

'Isn't it exciting?' enthused Cleo.

'Yes,' said Jade flatly. How could she get excited about some stupid TV show when her whole life was in pieces?

'So who do you reckon is likely to get picked?' Cleo babbled on, realizing that her attempts to cheer Jade up were failing miserably. 'Do you reckon Tansy is in with a chance?'

'How the hell should I know!' shouted Jade. 'What does it matter anyway?'

'Sorry,' muttered Cleo.

Why did I say that? thought Jade. What's wrong with me? Why am I becoming so horrid?

'Jade, I'm sorry about you and Scott, honestly I am.' Cleo sounded really concerned and for one instant, Jade wanted to pour out everything.

'Poor you,' added Cleo.

Suddenly Jade had had enough. Poor Jade, whose parents got killed. Poor Jade, who had to leave her home and all her friends in Sussex. Poor Jade, who can't even hang on to a guy. She was fed up of pity. She wanted to be like everyone else.

'It's no big deal,' she said. 'Who cares about some naff guy who flips over the slightest thing?'

Even as she said it, she knew she didn't mean it. She just couldn't help it.

There was a long pause at the other end of the phone.

'Well,' Cleo said eventually, 'I've got to go. Trig's coming round later – and Mum will go ballistic if I haven't done my homework first. See you tomorrow.'

When Cleo had hung up, Jade stood for a long time staring into space. Tomorrow. She knew what it would be like. Everyone would be quizzing her about what had happened between her and Scott. Her friends would try to be nice and that would make her want to cry. On the other hand, if Scott really had told them everything, they would be thinking she was really horrid. Cleo probably thought she was the pits. She hadn't meant to snap. It was just that she felt so miserable and fed up and alone.

She dragged herself upstairs to finish her homework. Some stupid English essay entitled 'If only . . .' that she was meant to finish a week ago. *If only I hadn't said those things; if only Mum and Dad were here; if only I didn't have to go to school tomorrow.*

8.55 p.m. Ambitious and able

'Tansy Meadows, superstar!' Tansy answered the phone, sure that it was Holly phoning back. 'Oh, sorry, Mrs Vine – I thought it was Holly . . . Yes, fine thanks – I'll get her for you.'

She crashed into the sitting room where her mother and Laurence were watching *The Bridges of Madison County*. Clarity was sprawled across Laurence's lap in a manner which Tansy considered deeply unsuitable for someone of her age.

'Holly's mum's on the phone for you,' she said curtly, noting with disgust the way Laurence was playing with her mother's hair and kissing the top of her head. 'So if you could put each other down for a minute . . .'

Clarity grinned, totally unmoved by her daughter's disapproval, and pressed the pause button on the video. Meryl Streep and Clint Eastwood froze in an embrace on the screen. *Everyone*, thought Tansy, *is at it. Except me.*

'So, how's school?' asked Laurence when Clarity had gone to take the call.

'That', declared Tansy, wondering how anyone could possibly go out in a blue cord shirt and brown trousers and not be arrested, 'is the most naff question anyone can ask. But since you ask, it's as good as it gets.'

Laurence pursed his lips and clasped his hands together as if in prayer.

'And what do you want to do when you leave the place?'

Tansy stared at him. How weird that he should ask that question just now, when she had spent all day thinking of little else. Not that it was any of his business – but still, she could sound him out. It would be good practice.

'I want to be an archivist,' she said, and took great satisfaction in watching Laurence's amazed expression.

He cleared his throat.

'And do you know what an archivist is?' he asked.

Tansy raised her eyebrows.

'Oh no, that's why I want to be one,' she snapped. 'They find out about the past, trace family histories, all that sort of stuff.'

'That's right,' said Laurence. 'That's a very unusual ambition.'

Oh whoopee, thought Tansy. Perhaps he's not as pompous as I thought.

'Of course, I know a great deal about all that sort of thing,' he assured her.

Yes he is, she observed.

He took a notebook and pencil from his trouser pocket and began scribbling.

'I'll get you some books from the library – you can read up on it. Now what you probably don't know is this –'

Tansy was about to make her escape when Clarity burst into the room.

'Guess what?' she said with a grin.

'We've won the Lottery?' asked Tansy hopefully.

'No, silly – Holly's mum wants me to quote for redesigning their garden. I'm going for coffee tomorrow.'

It is, thought Tansy, utterly amazing what excites some people.

TUESDAY

8.10 a.m. Guess who's here again?

'Oh, Tansy,' said her mother, peering out of the sitting-room window. 'Look who's here!'

She made it sound as if Brad Pitt had put in an appearance outside their door. Sadly, as Tansy followed her mother's gaze, she saw it was only Andy Richards, duffel bag in one hand and trainer laces flapping, who was crossing the road to their front door.

'Get rid of him, Mum!' hissed Tansy urgently. 'Tell him I've left.'

'Don't be silly, darling,' said her mother. 'I did that yesterday. It's very rude.'

'Mum! Just get rid of him!'

It was too late. Clarity had opened the front door and was standing on the step with the sort of smile normally reserved for visiting royalty.

'Morning!' she said brightly. 'Have you come for

47

Tansy? Do come in.'

Tansy cringed.

Andy stepped into the room looking a little sheepish.

'Hi,' he said. 'I thought we could walk to school.'

Clarity looked unaccountably pleased.

'Brilliant idea!' she cried as if Andy had just mapped out plans for the next moon landing. 'Off you go, sweetheart – have fun!'

She planted a kiss on Tansy's forehead.

I think, thought Tansy, I might quite like to die now.

'Your mum's really nice,' said Andy as Tansy stomped along beside him in stony silence. 'What does she do?'

'Gardening,' said Tansy curtly. And makes a profession out of embarrassing me, she thought, grimly.

'And what about your dad?' persisted Andy, flicking a wayward strand of brown hair out of his eyes.

Oh no, thought Tansy. You're not getting me on to that subject.

'What is it with you?' she snapped. 'You want a rundown of all my relatives?'

Andy looked mortified.

'Sorry,' he said. 'I just wondered.'

'He left when I was a baby, OK?' she said abruptly.

Andy frowned and shoved his hands deeper into his pockets.

'That's tough,' he said, in the sort of voice that suggested he wasn't in the least shocked. 'Still, at least you don't remember him. That makes it easier.'

Tansy turned on him.

'Easier!' she expostulated. 'Easier than what? And anyway what would you know about anything?'

Andy chewed his bottom lip and pushed his glasses up the bridge of his nose.

'My mum left. Last year. I haven't seen her since and I don't know where she is. She just went.'

Tansy felt the pits. She couldn't imagine what that must be like. At least she'd never known her father but her mum was everything. Without her – it didn't bear thinking about.

'I'm sorry,' she said. 'Really.'

Andy looked at her and nodded slowly.

'It's OK,' he said. 'She'll be back one day. I'm sure she will.'

It occurred to Tansy that he didn't seem too sure at all.

9.00 a.m. Registration

'Hi, Jade, are you OK?' Tansy touched her friend on the shoulder.

'Yes, why shouldn't I be?' replied Jade shortly. When people were nice to her, she wanted to cry.

'What happened yesterday?' persisted Tansy, noticing how pale and drawn Jade was looking.

Jade shrugged.

'You mean apart from you lot almost landing me in it with Paula?' she said. 'She said you phoned to find out where I was.'

Tansy nodded.

'But once we realized that she thought you were at school, we wriggled out of it,' she pointed out. 'We were worried, though.'

Jade gave a half smile. Maybe Scott hadn't said too much after all.

'Well, don't be. I just took a day off to chill, OK? I'm fine now.'

It occurred to Tansy that she had never seen Jade looking less fine. She would have asked more but the bell rang for first period.

9.45 a.m. On the trail

Holly was sitting in Maths, wondering why on earth it was necessary to know the percentage profit some mythical greengrocer made on his tomatoes, when Mr Boardman, the headmaster, came striding into the classroom, followed by a tall, lean woman with a pointed chin, enormous scarlet-rimmed spectacles and a pair of bright-yellow fish earrings.

Amid much scraping of chairs and dropping of pencils, 9C stood up. Mr Boardman was very hot on what he called the finer points of old-fashioned etiquette.

'Good morning, 9C,' he boomed, beaming at

50

them with the caring expression reserved for use in front of parents, governors and visitors. 'Excuse me for interrupting your class, Mrs Bainbridge, but I would like to introduce Frau Dimmerstucker from Hamburg. She is here to observe English teaching methods as part of a report she is writing for the European Parliament.'

A stranger! Holly's brain went on red alert.

Mrs Bainbridge beamed at the visitor and held out her hand.

'How nice to meet you!' she simpered.

'I very much would like to watch you in zis class,' said the visitor. 'It is for me very good zat I see ze way of teaching is zis countreee.'

Oh puh-leese, thought Holly, that accent! Naff, or what? You're no German – you're a spy for *GFI!*

Her heart raced with excitement. She had to let the others know that she had it sussed already. And she had to make sure that Frau so-called Dimmerstucker noticed her.

'Miss Dimmerstucker will be sitting in on a number of lessons over the next couple of days,' announced Mr Boardman, turning to face the class. 'And I trust you will give her all the help she needs.'

You bet, thought Holly. I shall be charm itself. Because I know who she really is. She doesn't fool me one little bit.

Tansy hugged herself in excitement. Only Tuesday, and already she knew exactly who the guy from

GFI! was! Just wait till she told the others. Of course Mr Boardman had passed him off as a photo-journalist taking pictures for a book called *The Teenager Observed*, but Tansy wasn't stupid enough to be taken in by that garbage. It was obvious; all the observing that Phil Douglas was doing was not for a non-existent book, but to spot some kids for the show. And now that Tansy knew that, she was going to make sure that his lens focused on her as much as possible.

And she would make sure she got to chat to this guy. Soon. And let slip about her ambition. Or at least – just enough to get her on the show. The rest could wait. For now.

Cleo was feeling all tingly. She was only in the same set as Trig for two subjects – English and History – and he sat just in front of her, which meant she could gaze at the way his hair curled into the nape of his neck, but did little for her ability to concentrate on the War Poets.

At the end of English, he turned to her with a somewhat desperate look on his face.

'I need your help,' he confessed.

Cleo, who liked nothing better than feeling needed, felt a warm glow.

'It's my English homework,' Trig continued. 'It was supposed to be in last week and now Birdie says if I don't hand it in tomorrow, I'll get detention. I haven't a clue what to write. It's a dumb subject anyway.'

Trig always got sullen when he was worried.

'Is it that "Twenty Years On" thing she gave us last week?' asked Cleo.

Trig nodded.

'I'm useless at that sort of stuff,' admitted Cleo. 'I did a thing about what Dunchester might be like in twenty years' time. You know, monorails and shopping by TV, that sort of thing. But I guess you're more interested in the past than in the future!'

Trig nodded.

'The further back the better,' he said.

'Do you really want to be an archaeologist?' she asked.

'You know I do – why?'

Cleo couldn't tell him about *GFI!* but she needed to know more.

'I just wondered what the fascination with digging up bits of pottery could possibly be,' she said teasingly.

'Oh, so you think I'm a weirdo too, do you?' Trig snapped. 'Why don't you just come right out and say so?'

Cleo gulped. Trig always got defensive if he thought someone was sending him up.

'I don't – I just wanted . . . I mean, I just like to know what makes you tick.'

'What – so you can snigger about me to all your

mates?' Trig slammed his textbook into his bag.

'Hey, hang on!' Cleo was beginning to get cross. 'What is it with you? No one thinks being an archaeologist is naff – half of them don't know what one does anyway. Can't I show an interest without getting my head bitten off?'

Trig looked contrite.

'Sorry,' he mumbled.

He picked up his bag and turned to face Cleo.

'It's like putting a jigsaw together – finding out all the bits of the past that have got lost and buried, and making it all into some kind of sense. And then there's always the chance . . .'

He stopped.

'Go on,' urged Cleo.

'Well,' Trig said in a rush, 'I might just discover something really big, like the guy that found Tutankhamun's treasures and then I'd be really famous.'

He grinned, his bad mood evaporating.

'I might even get to make one of those documentaries – *Lost Civilizations* or something,' he said. 'I can see myself in the white jacket and Ray-bans, telling the world about my latest discoveries! You never know – in twenty years' time you might be watching me on TV!'

Hopefully it won't take twenty years, thought Cleo, itching to tell Trig about *GFI!*

'There you are then,' she said instead.

'What?' Trig frowned.

'Twenty years on – write about what you will be doing twenty years from now! That way you get to write about archaeology which you find easy anyway, and . . .'

She stopped. An amazing thought had just hit her.

'That's a brill idea!' exclaimed Trig, grabbing his books. 'See you later.'

'Mmm,' murmured Cleo.

It couldn't be, could it? Perhaps she should tell the others. But then again she often got things wrong and she didn't want to look an idiot.

And besides, if she was right, it was too late for anyone to do anything about it.

12.30 p.m. Lingering over lunch

'Where's Jade?' Holly dumped her plate of burger and beans on the table and glanced round the cafeteria. She wanted to be sure that all three of her friends heard her news.

'Getting some food – I wish she'd hurry up,' said Tansy, wriggling on her seat with excitement at her discovery.

'Did you find out what happened yesterday?' asked Cleo anxiously. 'She was pretty vague on the phone.'

Tansy shook her head.

'I tried talking to her in Registration,' she said. 'But she was pretty short with me. Sssh – she's coming.'

They're talking about me, I know they are, thought Jade miserably, balancing a bowl of soup and a roll on her tray. They're probably saying that I'm the pits and they don't want anything more to do with me.

'Hi, Jade,' said Holly brightly. 'You OK?'

'Why shouldn't I be?' said Jade and then wished she hadn't. She stared gloomily at her vegetable soup.

'No reason,' said Holly placidly. 'Anyway, you lot, just listen to this.'

'Hang on,' said Tansy. 'What I've got to tell you is mega important.'

'Not compared with this,' interrupted Holly. 'Guess who I've seen?'

'Who?' asked Cleo through a mouthful of macaroni cheese.

'The researcher from you know what,' stressed Holly.

Tansy felt decidedly irritated. She thought she was the only one to have it sussed.

'She's posing as some German woman,' said Holly. 'But that is obviously just a front. She even calls herself Frau Dimmerstucker!'

'Unreal!' said Tansy. 'Well, they must have sent two people down because I have definitely sussed out someone.'

Cleo and Holly stared at her. Jade went on stirring her soup absent-mindedly.

'He's called Phil Douglas and he's supposedly

taking pictures for some book about teenagers,' she said, unwrapping a cheese slice. 'But it's pretty obvious that's just a cover to allow him to walk round school with a camera.'

'Brilliant!' exclaimed Holly, spilling baked beans down her shirt in her excitement. 'Now we know who they are, we need to make absolutely sure they notice us.'

Cleo looked thoughtful.

'I was just wondering', she ventured, 'whether you are both wasting your time. You see, I –'

Tansy looked irritated.

'Of course we're not,' she said. 'You always look for the problems, Cleo. You may not want to get on the show but Holly and I do. Just because you're not interested –'

Cleo gulped.

'I am, I am,' she insisted. And kept quiet. After all, she was probably wrong.

WEDNESDAY

7.30 a.m. Relative surprises

Tansy was clattering downstairs for breakfast when the telephone rang. Her mother picked up the receiver just as Tansy opened the kitchen door.

'Dunchester five-seven-seven-zero-seven-eight . . . Beth! What a surprise!'

Tansy stopped. Beth must have got the letter. Brilliant!

Only not so brilliant if she let on about it to Mum. She realized with a jolt that she hadn't told Beth to keep it a secret.

'Can I talk to her?' she said quickly, hand out-stretched. Her mother shook her head impatiently and turned her back.

Tansy prayed hard.

'What's that, Beth . . . Really? What, in Dunchester? Terrific!'

Tansy held her breath.

'Today! Better still! Of course, love to see you. I get back from work about five . . . I'll leave a key in the plant pot by the front door . . . Wonderful. Ciao!'

Clarity put the phone down and turned to Tansy with a broad grin on her face.

'Beth's coming up for a couple of days!' she exclaimed. 'New boyfriend's up here working for a bit, she's got some holiday owing and felt like seeing us both. Isn't that great?'

Tansy nodded eagerly. Beth must, absolutely must, know something. People don't bomb up motorways for no reason and the story about boyfriends and holidays was just a ruse. She was so excited that she could hear her heart beating in her ears. Things were starting to happen.

She was just about to leave for school when Laurence loped through the back door with a broad grin on his face.

'Oh, you're still here, Tansy,' he said.

'That is stating the obvious,' commented Tansy dryly.

'Tansy!' Her mother did not see the funny side. 'Hi, Larry.'

She gave him an unnecessarily lengthy kiss and Laurence ruffled her hair as if she was a small child and wiggled her nose with his finger.

Why is it, thought Tansy, that when my mother talks to any man she goes all pink and pathetic?

'Coffee? Tea? Can I cook you some breakfast?' asked Clarity.

Heaven preserve us, thought Tansy. She'll be lying down and inviting him to walk all over her next.

'No thanks,' said Laurence, flicking his unspeakable fringe out of his eyes and beaming at Tansy. 'I just brought these round for Tansy. Those books I was talking about.'

He handed her a couple of paperbacks.

'Thanks,' said Tansy. Much as it annoyed her to admit it, these might be pretty helpful when it came to impressing the *GFI!* people.

'Oh, and there's this one,' he said, passing her a crumpled carrier bag. 'You might have fun with this.'

He handed her a big hardback book, with a card sticking out of the top, covered in spidery handwriting.

Tansy,
I thought you might like to browse through this. I gather it's a cult thing with your age. The quizzes at the back are fun — if you get stuck, ask me. I'm pretty hot on general knowledge.

Enjoy!
Laurence

Conceited git, thought Tansy reading the note. And then looked at the cover of the book. The heart-stopping features of Ben Bolter gazed up at her.

It was the all new *Go For It! Annual*. It had to be an omen. It just had to be.

Phil Douglas certainly got round the school with his camera. Tansy beamed at him in the Science lab while he snapped away at kids with Bunsen burners and angled her computer screen to show her best profile during Computer Studies.

Unfortunately, he wasn't around during hockey practice, which was a bit of a downer since she scored two goals but her moment came during the last period of the afternoon when she spotted him sitting on a bench outside the gym.

'Hi, Mr Douglas,' she said. 'Are you getting loads of good pictures?'

'Pretty good, I guess,' said Phil, unscrewing one lens and fitting another. 'The worst part about it is having so short a time to work in. The headmaster is only letting me stay for a couple of days.'

That fits, thought Tansy.

'Do you think I am photogenic?' she asked, inclining her head to one side and hoping that she looked sophisticated.

Phil grinned and ran his fingers through his curly black hair.

'That's what all you girls want to know,' he said. 'I bet you want to be a supermodel!'

Bad move, thought Tansy. That's been done to death.

'Oh no,' she said hastily. 'My ambitions are far bigger than that. I want to be an archivist, a family historian, a genealogist . . .' She quoted all the words she could remember from the books that Laurence had given her, and which she had been reading during study period when she should have been learning French verbs.

'Now that really *is* interesting!' said Phil, impressed. 'Why would you want to do that?'

This is it, thought Tansy. I've got to get this right. And couldn't think of a thing to say that wouldn't give the game away.

'I just think it really matters that you know where you came from,' she said lamely. 'And not everyone does. I'd like to run a company that found people – I mean, found out about people.'

That came out all wrong, she thought miserably.

'That', said Phil, 'is one hell of a bright idea. Good on you. I hope it works out for you.'

'So you like the idea?' Tansy pressed, hope rising.

Phil looked surprised.

'Yes . . . not that it is anything to do with me,' he said.

'Of course not,' said Tansy knowingly. 'Of course not.'

Cleo was getting more and more certain that her idea was the right one. Frau Dimmerstucker had hardly shown a glimmer of interest when Cleo told her that there was this Year Nine guy who wanted to be an archaeologist, and her ring binder was full of pretty official-looking papers with rubber stamp marks all over them.

And when Phil Douglas interrupted their CDT lesson to take pictures, she dropped big hints about ambitions and careers, but he just told her she had fascinating bone structure and took her picture while she made papier mâché.

There was no doubt in Cleo's mind that the test had already been set. And not one of them had known about it.

2 p.m. Feeling miserable

Jade sat on a bench in the shopping arcade, picking half-heartedly at a packet of cheese-and-onion crisps. She had tried so hard. She had managed to get through Maths because she wasn't in the same set as Scott or any of her closest friends. She'd missed French by saying that she felt sick and had spent break sitting in the loo. But on her way to the Art block she had bumped into Scott in the corridor and, with her heart thumping in her chest, she had tried to make amends.

'Scott,' she had begun, 'about Saturday. I am really sorry.'

'I'm not,' he had retorted.

'You're not?' The relief had been enormous.

'No,' he retorted. 'At least now I know what you

are really like. So I'm not good enough for you?
Fine. You're not good enough for me either.'

And with that, he had stomped off down the
corridor.

When Jade had reached the Art block she had
walked straight on past the door, and then out of the
school gates. She knew she was being stupid, but
that didn't stop her. Half of her wanted to cry and
the other half wanted to smash something into a
zillion pieces. Right now she was angry with
everyone. Angry with Mum and Dad for dying;
angry with Paula for never talking about them;
angry with Scott for thinking all those things about
her which just weren't true. And most of all, angry
with herself for being like this.

She didn't know why she was being so horrid to
everyone. Especially now, when she wanted them all
to like her and be kind to her. For ages, her parents'
death had seemed like a bad dream, something
that she would wake up from and suddenly everything would be all right. But it was getting worse,
not better. She missed them more every day. She
wanted her mum right now, here, telling her that it
would be OK, that she loved her, that she would
take care of her. How could she just go and die?

Mum wouldn't think much of her skiving off
school. In fact, Mum would go ballistic. But Mum
wasn't here. No one really cared what happened
and neither did she. She threw the wrapper into the
bin and began walking again.

*

She was ambling down the hill, hoping that no one would notice her red eyes, when a silver-grey Granada pulled up beside her and a young woman with long dark hair wound down the passenger window.

'Excuse me,' she began. Jade pretended not to hear and quickened her pace.

'Excuse me, but can you tell me where West Green Upper School is?' the woman called again.

Just as Jade was taking a deep breath and attempting to look composed, a large woman with a poodle on a lead came the other way.

'Young of today – no manners at all,' she muttered, glaring in Jade's direction before turning to address the woman in the car. 'Can I help you at all, my dear?'

Jade sighed with relief and hurried to the other side of the road. The afternoon stretched ahead of her.

She didn't know what to do but one thing was certain – she wasn't going back to school.

She didn't notice Miss Partridge until it was too late.

'Jade? What on earth are you doing out of school?'

She looked up and there was her English teacher, dressed in a long, flowery skirt and pink angora sweater and looking like a small marshmallow.

Jade took a deep breath.

'Dentist,' she said.

Miss Partridge nodded slowly.

'And you've handed in a note?' she asked.

'Yes, miss,' Jade lied.

'Well,' said Miss Partridge decisively, 'I'm walking back to school. I'll keep you company.'

Oh terrific, thought Jade. Here comes the lecture.

But Miss Partridge merely chatted amiably about school and holidays and how her flat was being redecorated, and what fun it was to have a place of her own. She told her that she had just been out to book a skiing holiday with her boyfriend and how she did hope she would be able to stay upright because he had told her he was an expert skier.

Jade was just thinking that she had got away with it, when the teacher suddenly changed the subject.

'I suppose it feels to you as if nothing will ever be fun again,' she said conversationally, slowing her pace to allow for the steepness of the hill. 'No wonder you feel like getting away from it all, escaping.'

Jade stared at her.

'OK, OK,' said Miss Partridge. 'We'll stick with the dentist story for now if it helps.'

She smiled gently at Jade who relaxed just a little.

'My dad died when I was eleven, you know,' Miss Partridge added. 'It was awful.'

'I'm sorry,' whispered Jade. Her throat tightened as it always did when anyone mentioned death.

'I was so upset and I missed him,' said Miss

Partridge. 'And I was so very, very angry with him.'

Jade's eyes widened and she blinked back a tear.

'You felt angry too?' she asked. 'Really?'

'Furious,' asserted her teacher. 'I couldn't believe he'd just died and deserted me and my mother. Of course, I felt guilty for being cross and that just made it worse.' She paused while they crossed the road towards the school gates.

'My father used to encourage me so much – and I felt angry that he wasn't there to see me win a prize or get the lead in a school play. And I always told him I wanted to be a teacher – and do you know, even on the day of my first job, I was cross that he wasn't there to see me.'

Jade nodded slowly.

'My dad used to say that he'd be ill deliberately so I could nurse him,' she said with a faint smile. 'And Mum used to keep on about how I might be the first Williams to go to uni.'

She paused.

'You see, I've always wanted to be a doctor.'

Miss Partridge nodded.

'You mentioned that in your essay,' she said. 'I love the idea you had about injections being a thing of the past in twenty years' time. Cowards like me would much prefer your melting patches idea!'

Jade grinned.

'I'm probably too thick to be a doctor,' she said, 'but I will be a nurse. In Africa. Don't laugh,' she added hurriedly.

'Jade,' said Miss Partridge, 'why would I laugh? I think that's wonderful.'

She paused and leaned against the wall.

'And, Jade, you are not thick. You are very bright and capable. Saying you are thick is just another way of being angry with yourself. Anger has its place, Jade; grief, and loneliness and feeling scared – they are all OK. Running away isn't.'

She turned to her.

'All those feelings are inside you – when you run, they just come with you.'

That makes sense, thought Jade. I don't feel any better for having skived off. In fact, I feel worse.

'End of lecture,' said Miss Partridge briskly. 'It will get better, you know.'

Jade sighed.

'I wish it wasn't taking so long,' she said.

2.15 p.m. Late back

When Jade got back to school, Chemistry had already started.

'Oh, you've deigned to join us, Jade,' said Mr Cole sarcastically. 'And what pressing engagement causes you to be late for my class?'

'Sorry, sir,' said Jade meekly. 'I was talking to Miss Partridge.'

Mr Cole looked peeved.

'Oh,' he said, obviously irritated at being given a good excuse. 'Well, go over to the far table and join

Scott. We're carrying out the experiment on page seventy-six of your textbook.'

Jade took a deep breath. She was aware of at least six pairs of eyes watching her, Holly and Cleo's among them. She had no choice. She had to face him.

For a while she and Scott didn't say a word but merely set up their equipment and listened to Mr Cole droning on about heat conductors. They didn't look at each other.

This, thought Jade, is ridiculous.

'Look,' she said, taking a deep breath and feeling slightly sick, 'can we talk about things? I don't like –'

'Jade Williams!' Mr Cole snapped. 'Not only do you do me the discourtesy of turning up late, but now you see fit to talk instead of work! Go to that spare table and work on your own, where you cannot distract those who do come to school to learn!'

Jade heard a few muffled titters behind her. Why was everything in her whole life going wrong?

3.15 p.m. Holly makes progress

Holly was certain her moment had come. She was just clearing away her books after English, when Frau Dimmerstucker, who had been 'observing' the lesson from a seat at the back of the classroom, tapped her on the shoulder.

'I zort zat your reading of ze part of Viola was

very, very gut,' she said. 'You have a most musical speaking voice.'

Holly beamed and felt her cheeks glow. This was it. This was IT!

'Thank you, Frau Dimmerstucker,' she said in her most polite voice. 'I hope you are right – you see, I want to be a newsreader.'

The German woman's chin thrust itself forward in excitement.

'Sehr gut!' she cried. 'A child with ambition. I like zat!'

Holly was so thrilled that she didn't even mind being called a child. She had done it – she could feel it in her bones. It was only a matter of time before everyone would know that Holly Vine was going to be big on TV.

At home time, Holly couldn't contain her excitement. She knew she shouldn't say a word until it was absolutely definite, but it was so obvious that Frau Dimmerstucker had singled her out that when she spotted Cleo in the locker room she just had to tell her.

'So, you see,' she babbled after she had given her the news, 'I'm sure I'll be chosen. I can't wait.'

Cleo looked at her anxiously.

'Don't get your hopes up too much,' she began. 'I mean, Frau Dimmerstucker might not be . . . well, she might not have meant . . .'

'Oh, for heaven's sake, Cleo!' retorted Holly.

'Can't you just be glad for me? Do you always have to be such a wet blanket?'

Cleo gulped.

'Of course I'm glad,' she said hastily. 'That's terrific.'

I hope, she thought.

'What were you and Scott talking about when old Cole blew up?' asked Cleo as she walked home with Jade.

Jade bit her lip.

'*We* weren't talking about anything,' she said miserably. 'He doesn't want to know me any more.'

Cleo looked sympathetic.

'Poor you,' she said. 'Look, why don't you write him a note? You know – making up. I mean, he might walk off if you try talking to him, but he's bound to read a letter.'

Jade thought. It might work. But she didn't want to look as if she was grovelling.

'Oh . . . who cares?' she said, shrugging her shoulders and trying to look laid back.

'You do,' said Cleo. 'You don't fool me for one minute.'

4.00 p.m. Beth makes an entrance
Tansy sped down Weston Way and into Cattle Hill. Great! Her mother's disreputable van wasn't parked outside their cottage, which meant she was still at work.

She let herself in the front door and immediately knew that Beth had arrived. The smell of Eternity perfume pervaded the air and a number of expensive-looking carrier bags were dumped at the bottom of the stairs.

Tansy galloped up the stairs and knocked on the guest-room door.

'Hi, Tansy, how are *you*?' Beth opened her arms and gave her niece a bear-like hug. She wearing a snappy little navy suit and sling backs and looked a million dollars.

'Fine – it's so good to see you!' exclaimed Tansy, wishing she was tall and stylish. 'So you got my letter?'

'Letter?' Beth frowned and ran her fingers through her immaculately bobbed hair. 'No – mind you, I've been away for two days. Round at PJ's.'

'PJ?'

'The new guy in my life,' explained Beth. 'He is so cute – you'll die when you meet him. Hang on a minute – I went back and grabbed my post before we drove up.'

She rifled through her bag and pulled out a handful of mail.

'Bill, bill, junk, bill,' she muttered, flicking through the pile.

'That's the one,' said Tansy, pointing to a lime-green envelope. 'It's about my dad.'

Beth looked up.

'Your dad?' she said in surprise. 'Oh what, that Pongo person?'

Tansy's mouth dropped open and her mouth went dry.

'You mean, you know which one —'

She stopped as a car door slammed outside.

'That's Mum,' she said hastily. 'She doesn't know I've written – she gets upset . . .'

Beth gave her a quick hug.

'That's OK,' she said. 'I won't breathe a word. I'll read your letter and then we can talk later.'

'Promise?' Tansy had never been this close to knowing something about her dad before.

'Promise,' Beth assured her.

The front door slammed and Beth stuffed the letter into her handbag.

'Beth? Tansy? Are you there? I'm back!' Clarity's voice floated up the stairs.

'Coming!' Beth sped down the stairs.

Tansy followed more slowly.

Pongo. She had been right all along. So why had her mum said she didn't know who her father was?

4.30 p.m. Gossing
'So what's new, Tansy?' Beth asked.

They had spent the previous hour sitting round the kitchen table, eating huge wedges of carrot cake that Beth had brought up from Harrods food hall and opening the presents she had bought. She had given Clarity loads of expensive bath oils and body lotions in big glass bottles and Tansy a silver make-up bag packed with lip gloss, eyeliner and some wicked purple mascara, as well as a big and very expensive-looking bottle of Desire perfume.

'You shouldn't spend all this!' Clarity had exclaimed, uncomfortable that her little sister could produce gifts that would take her a month to save up for.

'I didn't,' Beth reassured her. 'They are all free-bies sent to the magazine – I'm drowning in smellies and potions, so you might as well have them.'

She nudged Tansy who was staring into space.

'Hey, you – you're miles away. So let's have all the goss – what's going on in your life?'

Tansy blinked. She had been thinking about fathers. And mothers who didn't tell you the truth.

'Not much,' she said. 'Oh, except that guess what? *GFI!* are coming to our school to choose kids.'

'What's *GF* . . . whatever you said?' asked her mum.

'*Go For It!*' interrupted Beth, who was far more into the current scene than Clarity. 'It's a big hit on cable – audience expanding every week.'

'Is that the programme with that guy you drool over?' asked Clarity.

Tansy pulled a face.

'Ben Bolter, yes it is!' she said. 'But I shouldn't

74

have said anything because no one is supposed to know they are coming until they turn up. Except that they have turned up and I know who they are.'

Beth raised an eyebrow.

'And no doubt you want to get on the show?' she said with a smile.

Tansy nodded.

'I think one of the research guys was mega impressed with my ideas,' she said confidently. 'What I came up with was this –'

She was about to tell Beth all about her idea when the doorbell rang.

'That'll be PJ,' cried Beth, leaping to her feet in excitement. 'Clarity, just wait till you see him. You will positively die!'

She ran to the front door and Tansy heard that sort of slurping sound that people make when they kiss so passionately that they appear to be eating one another.

'Come through and meet my sister and Tansy,' said Beth.

She appeared in the doorway, a little pink and dishevelled, holding the hand of a twenty-something guy with a huge grin and a mop of unruly black hair.

'This', she announced proudly, 'is PJ.'

Tansy turned round. And caught her breath.

'Well, hi there,' said PJ, holding out a hand. 'We meet again.'

Tansy's heart soared.

PJ was Phil Douglas. The TV guy. He was Beth's new man and he was here. In her house.

'Hi!' she said, giving him what she hoped was a winning smile. 'Great to see you again!'

If I play this one right, thought Tansy, I can't lose. *GFI!* here I come!

5 p.m. Preparing for Stardom

Tansy stood in front of her dressing-table mirror, casting a critical eye over her appearance. She thought that maybe she had gone just a little over the top with the styling wax, but when your hair was totally undisciplined at the best of times, it seemed sensible to make spikiness into a feature. She had gone to town with aubergine eyeliner and the new purple mascara and thought she looked quite sultry. She just hoped PJ would recognize latent talent when he saw it.

She was about to gallop down the stairs when she remembered that she was trying to look sophisticated. Pulling herself up to her full five-foot-one, she endeavoured to glide into the sitting room.

Beth was sitting in an armchair, with PJ on the floor beside her.

'So you've already met PJ, I hear,' she said, passing Tansy a glass of fruit juice. 'Has he captured you on film?'

PJ nodded.

'I have indeed,' he said. 'Although according to the headmaster, I'm not supposed to tell kids they've been snapped – he says it raises their hopes of fame!'

I knew it, thought Tansy. I absolutely knew it.

'Who else did you take pictures of?' she asked. It would help to know the competition.

'Oh, loads of kids,' PJ said airily. 'The thing is, at this stage, one needs –'

'Oh, come on,' urged Beth, scrambling to her feet. 'Enough work talk – what about this Chinese you said you owed me?'

PJ laughed.

'OK, OK,' he said. 'Bye, Tansy – nice to have met you. See more of you soon, no doubt.'

'You bet,' said Tansy.

And began planning what to wear on *GFI!*

7.00 p.m. Boy talk
'Hi, Tansy – it's me, Holly.'

Picking up the phone, Tansy was just about to tell Holly the amazing news when she thought better of it. It would only upset her friend and anyway, she would know soon enough.

'Listen,' Holly was gabbling on the other end of the phone. 'You know that family I told you about – the ones moving in to the new house at the end of our garden? Well, they have.'

'Have what?' asked Tansy.

'Moved in, silly,' said Holly. 'And these two guys

are to die for. Honestly, Tansy, they are totally gorgeous. They're twins only they don't look much alike. Apart from their legs. They have the most amazing legs.'

Tansy giggled.

'So are you about to vault over the fence and make advances on them?' she teased.

'Better than that,' said Holly excitedly. 'The boys go to Bishop Agnew College.' She named the posh private school in Dunchester.

'So?' said Tansy.

'And Bishop Agnew are sending a team to *GFI!* as well – so the boys will be in the audience, and I can get to chat them up.'

'Cool,' said Tansy. I wonder, she thought, whether these twins are as dishy as Todd. One thing was certain; they couldn't miss her. She was going to be the star of the show.

10.00 p.m. Past imperfect

'Tansy! Tansy, are you still awake?'

There was a knock on the bedroom door.

Tansy, interrupted from her daydream of winning *GFI!*, jumped up and opened the door. Beth, wearing a divine cream Joseph jacket and a jersey dress the colour of cappuccino coffee, gave her a conspiratorial wink and slipped into the room.

'PJ's gone back to the hotel – and Clarity's still out with the lurid Laurence,' she announced. 'My sister has a strange choice in men, doesn't she?'

Tansy sighed.

'Tell me about it,' she said. 'Why can't she choose someone like PJ? At least he's got a life.'

Beth flopped down on the bed and took off her jacket.

'Speaking of men, I read your letter,' she said. 'And this seemed like a good opportunity to talk. I don't know how much I can help. But I'll do what I can. Everyone has a right to know where they came from.'

Tansy looked at her gratefully.

'I know you were only little when Mum got pregnant,' she said. 'And I know you won't have been told anything but –'

'Hang on,' said Beth. 'I had to listen to heaps and heaps.'

'What?' Tansy gasped.

Beth clasped her hands behind her head and closed her eyes.

'I was only seven when Clarity left home,' she said. 'And when she came back, she had to share my bedroom for a while because Mum had turned her old room into a study. So she would lie in bed and talk to me. Well, more to herself really – I guess she thought an eight-year-old wouldn't take much notice. But I did. I hung on her every word.'

Tansy's heart quickened.

'And?'

Beth screwed up her face in thought.

'She went on a lot about a guy called Jordan who was really arty and who painted flowers and birds on pebbles and sold them in the local craft shops,' she recalled. 'She said she was in love with him, but he went off with someone else and she was devastated.'

Beth paused and looked at Tansy.

'I remember thinking how sad and how romantic it was – you know, like you do when you're a kid.'

Tansy nodded.

'Clarity was really miserable. She was homesick but didn't want to admit that she had been silly to leave home. I remember she told me the story, over and over, how one day she was walking on the hills and couldn't stop crying. And that's where Pongo found her.'

'And they . . . well, you know . . .' said Tansy.

Beth nodded.

'They became an item. As a kid, I thought it so romantic but I reckon it must have been awful.'

'How come?' asked Tansy.

'A couple of weeks later, Pongo told her that he was engaged to a girl back in Illinois.'

Tansy involuntarily clamped her hand to her mouth.

'He said his time with Clarity was just a bit of fun, no big deal, and that he was going back to the States the following day,' continued Beth, kicking off her shoes and tucking her feet under Tansy's duvet. 'He left – and a few weeks later your mum discovered she was pregnant.'

Tansy cupped her chin in her hands and stared at Beth.

'So she really doesn't know which one my dad is?' she sighed. 'But when I mentioned my father to you, you immediately said Pongo.'

Beth nodded.

'It was the photograph, I suppose,' she said. 'She had these pictures and as soon as you were born it was pretty obvious that you were Pongo's daughter. You are the image of him – same shaped face, same colouring, everything.'

Tansy caught her breath.

'Photograph?' she gasped, her mind racing. 'I've never seen a photograph.'

Beth shook her head.

'I don't suppose you would have done,' she said. 'Clarity knew that by the time you were born, Pongo would be married to this American girl. She didn't have an address for him, and for some reason she didn't want to let on that she was having his baby. She couldn't tell you that Jordan was your dad, when she knew it wasn't true, so she decided to say she didn't know.'

Tansy couldn't understand quite why, but she wanted to cry. Not that she ever cried in front of anyone, least of all Beth who was so together and sophisticated.

81

So why were tears trickling down her cheeks? And why couldn't she stop?

Beth wrapped her arms around her and gave her a hug.

'It's hard, isn't it?' she said, offering Tansy a tissue.

Tansy nodded, sniffed and blew her nose.

'Am I stupid to want to meet my dad so much?' she sobbed, her shoulders shaking. 'To know what he's like and how he talks and everything? Do you think that's crazy?'

'Of course not,' said Beth. 'It's perfectly natural – he's part of you, after all.'

Tansy wiped her eyes.

'He might have kids – I might have half-brothers and sisters, and I'll never know.'

Beth sighed.

'Maybe it's best that way,' she said. Tansy sniffed. She wasn't sure that she agreed.

'I wish I had a photograph – that would be better than nothing,' she said.

Beth bit her lip.

'I remember that your mum had this tapestry bag. She kept secret stuff in it. I know that because she yelled at me once when I touched it. The pictures were in that.'

Beth paused and looked hard at Tansy.

'I probably shouldn't say this,' she said, 'but I know my sister. There is no way she would ever throw those pictures away. No way at all.'

Tansy stared at her.

'One thing is certain,' concluded Beth. 'Those photographs must be somewhere in this house. All you have to do is find them.'

The one advantage of having an aunt who was only eight years older than you, thought Tansy, was that she's still young enough to think up scams. They had got it all sorted. Beth was going to meet Clarity from work the following day and take her shopping.

'Knowing your mum it will probably be wind chimes and organic carrots,' laughed Beth. 'But I'll do my best to keep her out of the way while you have a root around for the pictures.'

After Beth had gone to bed, Tansy lay awake wondering where the photos could be. The cottage was tiny and Clarity was always complaining that there was nowhere to put anything. She kept on saying that when she got a really big garden design commission, they would have the loft converted and then they could . . . the loft! That's where she'd look. They must be in the loft.

Suddenly Tansy needed to see that picture more than anything else on earth. Even getting on to *GFI!* seemed unimportant by comparison. Although . . .

Tansy sat bolt upright in bed. She couldn't! Could she? It might just work. If she had a photograph of her father and the whole world was watching *GFI!* Yes! That was it.

If only she could manage to see it through.

THURSDAY

'It has to be today!' whispered Tansy to Holly as they filed into the school hall for Assembly. 'The show's on Saturday so they can't leave it any longer to make the announcement.'

Holly nodded in agreement. She just hoped that Tansy wouldn't be too jealous when she got picked for the show.

Cleo, who was just behind them talking to Jade, glanced at the platform. Mr Boardman was ushering a young woman and a tall thin man to chairs beside him.

'Who are they?' she hissed to Jade.

Jade looked across the room and frowned. There was something familiar about the woman. She had seen her somewhere before, quite recently. But she couldn't think where.

'Good morning, everybody!' boomed Mr Boardman.

84

'Good morning, sir,' they chanted respectfully.

'Now, before we begin I want to give you all an exciting piece of news. West Green has been chosen to appear on *Go For It!* this very Saturday.'

The whole hall erupted into a babble of sound and he held up his hand for silence.

Tansy nudged Holly.

'Where are the so-called Frau and PJ?' she whispered.

Holly shrugged.

'You will recall that we set you some essays last week,' Mr Boardman continued. 'Some of you were given the title "If Only", and others "Twenty Years On".'

I was right, thought Cleo. I knew I was right.

'Well, with me today I have two researchers from *GFI!* – and they've read all your work and chosen West Green's team!'

Tansy gasped. What about PJ? He'd said he was . . . no, he hadn't. He hadn't actually said anything about television. Surely he wasn't really doing all that snapping for a book after all?

Holly's heart was sinking. If Frau Dimmerstucker really was a German, all that effort had gone to waste.

Jade suddenly realized where she had seen the woman – in the car asking the way to school. If only she had guessed, she could have warned the others.

'And now', said Mr Boardman, holding up his

hand for silence, and picking up a red folder, 'for the big moment. Just who has been picked to appear on *Go For It!*?'

Tansy held her breath and crossed her fingers.

Holly told God that if he let her get on the show she would never, ever do anything horrid ever again.

Cleo willed them to read out Trig's name.

Jade was trying to work out what to say in her letter to Scott, the last ten attempts at which she had torn up in disgust.

'Over to the *GFI!* team,' said Mr Boardman.

Oh, get on with it, thought Tansy.

The girl with the ponytail stood up.

'Hi,' she said brightly. 'I'm Val Porter, and I'm a researcher for *GFI!*'

Get on, urged Tansy silently.

'We've picked six people,' she said. 'Four from Year Nine and two from Year Ten.'

The hall fell silent.

'Andy Richards, who wants to be an investigative journalist,' she began. A cheer went up from Andy's mates. Tansy couldn't believe it. She had no idea Andy was ambitious. She liked ambition in a guy.

'Abigail Reilly – marine biologist; Matthew Santer – jockey; Trig Roscoe – archaeologist . . .'

'Yessssss!' said Cleo. And turned scarlet as everyone around her burst out laughing.

Please, please, God, prayed Holly.

'Ursula Newley – she wants to dance with the National Ballet.'

Holly felt sick. Only one more name to go. Tansy wanted to cry. If only she had known that the essay was for the show, she would have worked a zillion times harder.

'And finally . . .'

You could have heard a pin drop.

'Tansy Meadows! A lovely essay about helping people to find their roots. She'd like to be a genealogist.'

Holly swallowed, closed her eyes, opened them again, and put a smile firmly on her lips.

'Well done!' she said, trying desperately not to feel insanely jealous.

Tansy's eyes were unusually bright.

'Thanks,' she whispered.

She'd done it! She had really done it! Now all she had to do was get to the final and her whole life could be transformed. She was so excited that she began to feel sick.

'And lastly,' said the researcher, holding up her hand to silence the chattering pupils. 'We have two names as reserves – just in case any of the team fall ill. And these are . . .'

Me, me, me, Holly pleaded silently.

'Jade Williams and Scott Hamill. Jade hopes to nurse in Africa, and Scott wants to be a sports commentator.'

Jade's mouth dropped open in amazement. Cleo hugged her. Tansy grinned.

Holly turned away.

Not only had Jade got the guy Holly fancied but now she had all the limelight as well. Life was distinctly unfair.

Jade, meanwhile, was in a daze. She would get a whole day with Scott. A whole day in which he would ignore her existence.

She couldn't bear it.

She would have to write him that letter. And soon.

While Tansy was relishing the thought of forthcoming fame, her mother was sitting at Angela Vine's kitchen table silently doing sums. She mustn't undercharge, or Angela would think she didn't know what she was doing, but then if she overcharged, she wouldn't get the job.

'I think', she said tentatively, 'that I could do what you want for nine hundred and eighty pounds.' That sounded so much less than a thousand, she thought.

'Oh, wonderful!' Holly's mother clapped her hands in glee. 'When can you start?'

'The week after next?' suggested Clarity, and then hesitated. 'Oh – that's half term. I don't really like leaving Tansy every day . . .'

She paused.

'No problem,' said Angela, waving a hand in the air. 'She can come and spend time with Holly. Such a lovely girl, your daughter. You must be very proud of her.'

'Yes,' said Clarity. 'Yes I am.'

The problem is, she thought, that right now I don't think Tansy is very proud of me.

'It can't be easy bringing a child up on your own,' commented Angela, pouring more coffee from the cafetière.

'It's not,' admitted Clarity.

'It's none of my business,' said Angela, who made a profession out of sorting other people's lives, 'but when did you and her father split up?'

Clarity swallowed. She could tell the old story of him disappearing when she was a baby. She could say he died. But she was tired of stories.

'We were never together,' she said in a quiet, slightly shaky voice.

She raised her eyes.

Angela Vine was watching her closely.

'Tansy believes that I don't know who her father is,' Clarity said.

'But you do.' Angela Vine's remark was a statement, not a question.

She nodded.

'Yes,' she said. 'I do. And I have a feeling Tansy won't rest until she finds out.'

'Have another slice of ginger cake,' said Mrs Vine and settled down to listen.

2.05 p.m. Team spirit

'It's brilliant, you and me being on the team together, isn't it?' Andy beamed at Tansy as they gathered with the rest of the team to have their photographs taken for identity badges.

Tansy was so over the moon at being chosen that she felt kindly disposed to the entire universe.

'Great,' she smiled, as Val the producer handed out bright-green T-shirts with *GFI!* printed across the back in gold.

'I wish my mum could see me,' he said wistfully. 'Still, she might be watching somewhere, you never know.'

So might my dad, thought Tansy. Or at least someone who knows him. And if my plan works, we could be reunited really soon.

Val clapped her hands to attract everyone's attention.

'Your parents all signed consent forms when the school applied to take part,' said Val. 'And, of course, mums and dads can come along and watch the show.'

Mine can't, thought Jade and for a moment, the excitement faded. She knew Paula and David would come but it wasn't the same.

'Don't forget that for the first round, Go For Points, you are competing for your school and not yourselves,' explained Val. 'You play in pairs – we've put Tansy Meadows and Andy Richards together, Trig Roscoe and Abigail Reilly, and Matthew Santer with Ursula Newley.'

Andy tapped Tansy on the shoulder.

'I'm really glad it's you,' he said. 'Because I'm absolutely determined to win.'

Tansy looked at him in surprise. He sounded as if he really meant it. Perhaps he wasn't so drippy after all.

Except that he'd have to realize that he wasn't going to win the individual prize. She was.

2.55 p.m.

'Well, Jade, I expect you are secretly hoping someone falls by the wayside so that you can take part?' suggested Miss Partridge that afternoon, when Jade apologized for missing English.

'No way,' said Jade, shaking her head vigorously. 'I'd die of fright. I can't think why I was chosen in the first place – I mean, it's not as if I'm clever or anything.'

'Jade Williams!' exclaimed Miss Partridge in mock desperation. 'Will you stop running yourself down? Someone who wants to be a nurse in Africa needs faith in themselves. Oh, and by the way, I thought you might like to read this.'

She handed Jade a glossy hardback book called *Fever, Famine and Flame Trees*.

'I'd like it back when you've finished with it,' she said. 'It's about a mission hospital – I think you'll enjoy it and I'm sure it will give you something to think about.'

3.05 p.m.

Holly was trying very hard to feel happy for Tansy and Jade. But it wasn't easy. Now she and Cleo would be in the audience while the other two were stealing all the limelight. And even Cleo would have Trig to cheer for. Holly felt like a reject. Probably nothing exciting would ever happen in her whole life.

Never mind ambitions. She might as well become a nun.

4.15 p.m. Searching for the past

The moment Tansy got home, she flew upstairs, tore off her school uniform and pulled on her stonewashed jeans, an old sweatshirt and trainers. She reckoned she had about an hour to find the photographs and she wasn't going to waste a minute. It was even more vital than before that she found the picture of Pongo.

She grabbed a torch from her bedside drawer and went on to the landing. Pulling down the loft ladder, she clambered up the metal steps. The attic was so dark that she had to spend several minutes scrabbling around and waiting for her eyes to become accustomed to the dim light.

She hadn't realized that there was so much junk up here. There were boxes of books, and dozens of *Gardening Today* magazines. Her old rocking horse leaned lopsidedly against an artificial Christmas tree and a rusting doll's pram was propped beside some deckchairs.

'Think!' she told herself firmly. 'Where would she put them?'

Stacked against the wall were three battered suitcases. Tansy wrenched open one of them. It was full of baby clothes. Was I ever that small? thought Tansy in surprise.

The second was packed with blankets and old pillows but when she opened the third suitcase, she gave a sharp intake of breath. Underneath a pile of somewhat weird and wacky clothes was a small tapestry bag. As Tansy lifted it out, she realized that her hands were shaking.

She found it tucked at the bottom of the bag. It was bent at the edges, and there was a small tear on one side. Written on the back were the words:

Pongo – Somerset April 1984
At Tansy Fields

in fading blue ink.

The picture blurred as her eyes filled with tears. Her mother had known all along. She must have been named after the place and her mother hadn't even told her that. How could she? How could she?

For a long time after she had come down from the loft, Tansy sat on her bed, stroking the photograph with one finger. Beth had been right: the guy in the photograph was just like her. The same floppy hair, the same heart-shaped face. This was her father. Her dad. And no one had ever told her. And he was out there, somewhere in the world, not knowing she existed.

She had thought that when she found the photograph she would feel overjoyed, but instead she felt so angry it was like a physical pain in her chest. She would confront her mother the moment she got home. She would make her tell her the whole story, from start to finish.

And on Saturday . . . She stopped. If she said too much to her mother right now, she could very well blow her big idea for the TV show.

Maybe she should keep quiet for a bit longer. There was too much at stake to mess up now.

Tansy heard her mum slam the front door.

'Tansy, sweetheart? We're back!'

Tansy slipped the photograph into the pocket of her jeans and ran her fingers through her hair. For just a little while longer, she would act as if nothing had happened. She wiped her eyes on her sleeve, took a deep breath and went downstairs.

'Guess what!' she said, bursting into the kitchen and hoping she looked normal. 'I've been chosen for *Go For It!* on Saturday.'

'Wow!' breathed Beth. 'Clever you!'

'That's terrific!' exclaimed Clarity, giving her a hug. 'Oh, darling, I'm so thrilled for you! Can I come and watch?'

Tansy nodded. And then wondered whether after all that was such a good idea. Not that she could do anything.

'Yes, of course,' she said.

'Great,' beamed her mum. 'I'll bring Laurence.'

'Oh,' said Tansy, thinking that there were limits beyond which no teenager should be asked to go. 'Must you?'

'Yes,' said her mother. 'He'll love it.'

'Did you find it?' Beth whispered to Tansy while Clarity was in the kitchen preparing pasta for supper.

Tansy nodded.

'But don't tell Mum,' she pleaded. 'Please.'

Beth held up her hands in mock surrender.

'I won't say a word,' she said. 'Anyway, I'm off tomorrow morning early. PJ's going to be taking photographs at a rock concert and we've got free tickets.'

'Well, thanks for listening to me,' said Tansy. 'It's more than Mum ever does.'

Beth took her hand.

'Don't be too hard on her,' she said. 'Being a mum isn't easy.'

'Being a daughter isn't exactly a blast either,' sighed Tansy.

9.30 p.m. A romantic read

Jade was sitting up in bed, reading avidly. But it wasn't the book that Miss Partridge had lent her that was gripping her attention, but what she had found tucked inside one of the pages. It was a letter – or at least the second page of a letter. And it was very obviously a love letter.

which was wonderful.

You must never think I don't love you — how could I look at anyone else when I have you? Of course I wish I could see you every night — but you know I have to work late at least twice a week and after all, it is our future I am working for — the wonderful future we shall have together. You must realize how important my job is — frankly, the whole place would crumble without me.

You matter to me so much, my darling — I love everything about you. There has never been anyone like you before and never will be again.

By the way, don't keep telephoning me at work — it really is frowned upon and I have told you before how distracting it can be.

Just think — in a few months we shall be far away from here, just you and I together.

Take care, my sweetest Cuddles, and I will see you again very soon.

Your ever loving,
Pootle

Jade giggled. Pootle! And Cuddles! Wait till she told the others – they would die. The thought of Birdie in a passionate clinch was just bizarre!

She hugged herself and imagined her friends' faces when she told them. She'd have to work out what to do about the letter – should she tell Miss Partridge that she had found it and risk embarrassing her? Or just leave it in the book and pretend she hadn't seen it?

She'd ask the others. They'd know what to do.

Right now, she had more important things to do. She was going to write to Scott and try to explain her side of the story.

Then maybe, just maybe, by Saturday he would at least be speaking to her again.

FRIDAY

8.20 a.m. Birdie's boyfriend

Tansy arrived at school much earlier than usual, because Beth and PJ had given her a lift in PJ's cool convertible. Tansy decided that the day started off far better when you didn't arrive at school in the company of three bags of compost and a dozen small conifers.

She found Jade already sitting in their classroom, reading a book. She looked up as Tansy walked to her table and grinned.

'Hey, Tansy, I have to tell you – Birdie's in love!'

Tansy grinned back, pleased to see Jade looking happier.

'Birdie? How do you know?'

Jade beckoned her over.

'Look,' she said, handing Tansy the letter.

Tansy scanned the page.

'Pootle!' she exclaimed. 'Oh yuk! Pompous, more

98

like – he talks to her like she was a kid.' Suddenly Tansy's voice faded and a puzzled expression came over her face.

Jade laughed.

'Maybe she likes being bossed around – makes a change from doing it to us all day,' she said. 'What should I do though – should I give her the letter back or what?'

Tansy was staring hard at the page.

'Tansy? Tansy, are you listening?'

'Oh – sorry. What did you say?'

'I said, should I tell Miss Partridge about finding the letter?' repeated Jade.

Tansy frowned.

'I don't know,' she said distractedly. 'That writing – I've seen it somewhere before. You don't think it's one of the other teachers, do you?'

Jade peered over her shoulder.

'I don't recognize it,' she said. 'We could ask Cleo and Holly later.'

Tansy nodded.

'Best not say anything to Miss Partridge – well, not till *GFI!* is over, anyway. She will only get in a state.'

'OK,' said Jade, glad to have the decision taken out of her hands. 'Whatever.'

'Can you actually imagine Birdie in the throes of passion?' Holly giggled when Jade showed her the love letter during morning break.

'But it is romantic, isn't it?' sighed Jade. 'I mean, having someone think you are that wonderful?'

'Don't you think we should hand the letter back?' asked Cleo anxiously.

'Tansy said we shouldn't do anything until *GFI!* is over,' commented Jade. 'Because of getting Birdie all embarrassed.'

Cleo, who liked everyone to be happy all the time, nodded in agreement.

'OK,' she said. 'After all, it's no big deal.'

3.15 p.m. The penny drops

By the end of Friday afternoon, everyone was in a state of high excitement. All of Years Nine and Ten were going to be in the audience for the show, and there was a great deal of discussion among the girls about what they should wear just in case the amazing Ben Bolter actually spoke to them.

'Should I put my hair up, do you think?' Holly asked Cleo as they left the cafeteria after lunch. 'In case I have my photograph taken?'

And in case the amazing Bennett twins really do show, she thought.

'You won't,' said Cleo. 'You're not taking part.'

'She might,' Tansy said. 'You all might. They put pictures of all the school audiences in the annual each year. I'll show you.'

She scrabbled in her school bag and pulled out the *GFI!* annual that Laurence had given her. As she opened it, his card fell to the floor and she bent down to pick it up.

And froze.

As she stared at the handwriting, she knew at once where she had seen it before. It was identical to the writing on the letter which Jade had found in her book.

Laurence Murrin was Pootle. Laurence Murrin was Birdie's boyfriend. And what was worst of all, Laurence Murrin was two-timing Tansy's mum.

3.50 p.m. In contemplative mode

Tansy walked home deep in thought. In one blazer pocket was the card from Laurence and in the other, Miss Partridge's letter, which Tansy had slipped out of Jade's bag when her friend went to the loo.

How could her mum be so stupid? How come she hadn't sussed that Laurence had something to hide when he told her he could only see her two nights a week? What was it with her and men?

She took the letter out of her pocket and read it yet again. Quite what she was going to do with it she wasn't sure. She could tell her mum the whole story at once and get it over and done with. But even though her mother needed some firm talking to, she knew this was going to make her really miserable – and that would spoil the weekend and *GFI!*

Perhaps she should confront Laurence and get him to back off. Or she could just pretend she had never seen the letter and let things be.

But she knew she wouldn't do that. Her mum had a right to know before she made a fool of herself yet again. She was so useless at managing her love life that she needed Tansy to sort her out.

And once the show was over that was precisely what she would do.

4.15 p.m. Panic stations

Clarity was still at work when Tansy arrived home. She ran upstairs and rummaged through the debris on her bedroom floor to find her jeans.

Her jeans weren't there. She pulled open every drawer and scrabbled through the hangers in her wardrobe.

Where were they? And much more importantly, where was the photograph of Pongo? The photo she simply had to have with her for tomorrow.

She flew into the bathroom and pulled the lid off the wicker laundry basket. Her mum had probably had a clean up and chucked her jeans in, ready for washing on Monday. The basket was empty. Tansy suddenly felt incredibly sick.

4.20 p.m. In the kitchen

Tansy pulled open the door of the washing machine and pulled the jumble of damp clothes on to the floor. Tangled among the blouses and nightshirts were her jeans. She grabbed them and stuffed her hand into the pocket. As she touched a wad of soggy paper, her worst fears were confirmed.

Lying in her hand were the remains of the photograph of Pongo Price. The ink from the back had run, streaking what was left of the picture with blue smudges. As she tried desperately to smooth it out, it disintegrated into even more pieces.

The only thing she had to show her what her father was like had gone for good.

And without it, all her plans for tomorrow's show were shattered.

Tansy sat down on the kitchen floor, put her head on her knees and cried.

4.30 p.m. Totally tense

She was still sitting there, wearing her school clothes and holding the few remaining segments of Pongo's picture in her hand when her mum came home.

'Tansy! What on earth are you doing? And the washing – it's all over the floor. For heaven's sake, is this what I have to come home to after a tiring day!'

Suddenly Tansy had had enough. She jumped to her feet and shoved the damp paper into her pocket.

'You washed my jeans!' she shouted. 'You actually went into my room and took my clothes and washed them without asking! You had no right!'

Her mum raised an eyebrow and dumped her groceries on the table.

'If you fling clothes on the floor, you can't blame me for thinking they need washing,' she said. 'Your bedroom should carry a Government Health Warning.'

'Oh, that's right, make like it's my fault!' snarled Tansy, clenching her fists. 'You have no respect for my privacy.'

Clarity eyed her daughter suspiciously.

'You've been crying,' she said gently. 'Surely not over a pair of jeans?'

Tansy swallowed hard. She couldn't tell her mum about the photograph because then she would know Tansy had been searching through her stuff and go totally ballistic.

'Not just the jeans!' retorted Tansy. 'Everything. The way you treat me like some kid; the way you don't tell me about my father; the way you make a total idiot of yourself with a man who doesn't give a fig for you!'

Clarity sighed.

'Oh please, don't start on that all over again,' she pleaded. 'I can have a life too, you know. Laurence and I love one another and that's something you are simply going to have to accept.'

'Oh no, I'm not!' shouted Tansy, who was feeling such a mix of anger and misery that she didn't care what she said. 'Because Laurence doesn't love you at all. Not one little bit.'

Clarity's expression hardened.

'Tansy! That is enough!' she exploded. 'Since you are so keen that I should show you respect, maybe you would care to afford me the same privilege. You know nothing about Laurence or his feelings for me.'

Tansy glared at her.

'Well, that's where you are wrong!' she stormed. 'Look at that!'

And she pulled the love letter from her pocket and stuffed it under her mother's nose.

Clarity leaned against the fridge, her eyes scanning the scrawly handwriting. As she reached the end, the colour drained from her face and she bit her bottom lip.

'And where did you find this?' she asked Tansy in a whisper.

Tansy thought fast. If she told her mother the whole truth, Clarity would probably have a blazing row with Miss Partridge at the show, which would be too embarrassing to contemplate.

'Jade found it,' she said. At least that wasn't a lie.

Clarity pulled back her shoulders.

'Then it obviously is nothing to do with Laurence,' she said with obvious relief. 'It's just someone with similar handwriting. It's as simple as that.'

She didn't sound convinced.

'It's you that's simple!' yelled Tansy. 'Mum, can't you see? You're just doing it again – hurtling blindly into some stupid relationship before you know anything about the guy! What are you going to do? Carry on till you get pregnant and then tell some other kid that you haven't got a clue who her dad is! Won't you ever learn?'

Tansy had shouted so loudly that she began coughing. Clarity gripped the back of the kitchen chair and closed her eyes.

'That isn't fair,' she began.

'Oh, we're on to what's fair now, are we?' yelled Tansy. 'That's rich coming from you. Do you think it has been fair of you to pretend you hadn't a clue who my dad was when you knew it was Pongo all along?'

She stopped, heart thundering in her ears. She hadn't meant to say that – it had just come out.

Her mother stared at her but didn't say a word. Tansy noticed that she was clenching and unclenching her fists and breathing rapidly. Now Tansy had started, she couldn't stop.

'Oh yes,' she cried. 'I found out about the photograph.'

Her mother gasped and Tansy began sobbing again.

'Mum, why? Why didn't you tell me? Why?'

Clarity took a deep breath and locked her hands together.

'I want you to tell me how you got hold of the photograph,' she said evenly. 'And then I want you to give it back to me.'

Tansy felt awful. What could she do? She'd let it slip and now she would have to confess to her mother about what had happened.

'Beth said you had one and I found it in the attic,' she said.

'I see,' said her mother, 'so you have been rifling through my things. And you talk about privacy.'

'It's my FATHER, for heaven's sake!' yelled Tansy. 'I have a right to know.'

Clarity nodded slowly.

'OK,' she said at last. 'Give me the photograph and I'll try to explain.'

Tansy lowered her gaze.

'I haven't got it,' she said.

Her mother stared.

'Where is it?' she asked with icy calm. 'Answer me. Now.'

Tansy slipped her hand into her pocket and pulled out the fragments of damp paper. Opening her fist, she showed them to her mother.

For a moment, neither of them spoke. Tansy watched as her mother's eyes filled, and one solitary tear trickled slowly down her cheek.

Tansy felt awful. Mixed in with the anger towards her mum was a lump of guilt for having gone behind her back and made her cry, and misery at losing the only picture of her father she was ever likely to have. But it wasn't all her fault, was it?

'If you hadn't taken my jeans, the photograph would still be in one piece,' she muttered.

Suddenly her mother's composure snapped.

'Well, I hope you're satisfied!' Clarity shouted. 'You try to turn me against Laurence, you rummage through my things and you ruin my best photograph of the man I once loved. You had no right! No right at all!'

That did it.

'I have every right!' screeched Tansy. 'Everyone has the right to know where they came from. If you had been honest from the start, this need never have happened. It's all your fault for keeping secrets!'

'Oh, that's right, blame me!' she shouted. 'Blame me for doing my best for fourteen years, blame me for trying to think of other people, blame me for wanting to protect you – blame me, in fact, for everything, why don't you!'

And with that, she stormed out of the kitchen and ran up the stairs.

Tansy didn't move. She wished she could have the last ten minutes over again. She knew she'd handled it all wrong.

As she went slowly upstairs to change, she noticed the letter lying on the stairs where her mother had dropped it, and she picked it up. She thought she might need it. From behind her mother's closed bedroom door she heard the sound of sobbing. Tansy touched the doorknob, half wanting to go in and say she was sorry.

But why should she? Wasn't it up to her mum to apologize first?

It wasn't until she was lying on her stomach on the bed that a thought struck her.

Her mother had yelled at her for ruining her best photograph of Pongo. But if that had been the best, it meant there must be another one.

But it was too late to find it now.

7 p.m. Calming down

Tansy was staring out of the window, feeling miserable, when there was a knock on her door.

'Tansy, can I come in?' her mum called.

Tansy opened the door. Despite having red-rimmed eyes and tousled hair, Clarity gave her a watery smile.

'Come down and have some supper,' she said, trying to sound cheery and upbeat. 'It's spaghetti bolognese, your favourite.'

Tansy wanted to make her mother feel really guilty by saying that she was too upset to contemplate even a mouthful of food, but giving up spaghetti on a matter of principle was too much to ask even of her.

'Are you looking forward to tomorrow?' her mother asked brightly as they sat over their supper.

Tansy shrugged.

'I suppose,' she said. In fact, she *was* excited but didn't think that someone who had been so badly treated by a parent should let anything but abject misery show on their face.

Her mother laid down her fork and began fiddling with her serviette.

'Look,' she said in a rush, 'Laurence is coming to *GFI!* tomorrow and I don't want you to say anything to him.'

Tansy stared at her mother, a strand of half-sucked spaghetti hanging from her mouth. Laurence was going to have the audacity to go to the show, knowing Miss Partridge would be there! How could he? What kind of guy was this? He might think that neither of his two women knew about the other but he couldn't possibly imagine he was going to pull it off.

And her mother was still determined to believe nothing was going on. I've got to do something, thought Tansy. Mum may be totally insane but I don't want her hurt.

'Mum! You're crazy! You should be telling him where to go, not hanging out with him in public. You're . . .'

She stopped. Her mother's eyes were filled with tears and her lips were pressed firmly together.

'I'll handle it, Tansy,' she said softly but firmly. 'My way.'

She knows, thought Tansy. She knows that letter was from him. So why doesn't she phone and tell him where to go?

The workings of the parental mind were sometimes quite beyond her.

SATURDAY

Noon. Practice makes perfect?

Dunchester Leisure Centre was buzzing with noise as the teams broke for lunch. The whole morning had been spent rehearsing the games and being told what to do if you got knocked out of a round. Three other schools were taking part including Bishop Agnew College, the posh private school whose playing fields backed on to West Green's.

'Whatever happens,' said Tansy, as she and the others filed up to collect sandwiches and drinks, 'we have to slaughter them.'

'I'm determined to get to the final,' said Andy. 'I hope our team wins the school prize, but I really want the individual one. But then I guess we all do.'

'Not me,' said Jade. 'I just hope you all stay upright so I don't have to take part.'

'Me too,' said Scott spontaneously and then turned away, obviously annoyed that he had actually spoken to Jade. She took an envelope from her pocket and passed it to him, and before he could speak, moved off to chat to Cleo.

'What is the prize anyway?' asked Trig who, being newly arrived from America, had never seen the show.

'You get a whole day doing a job connected with your ambition,' said Andy. 'Last week a kid who wanted to be an airline pilot got to sit in the cockpit of a jet all the way to Malta and back.'

Trig looked impressed.

'You could get to go on a dig,' said Cleo, who had come across to wish them all good luck. 'And you'd get to work on a real newspaper, wouldn't you, Andy?'

Andy bit into his cheese roll.

'Actually, I don't want to be a journalist,' he admitted. 'I really want to be a merchant banker.'

'So why didn't you write about banking?' said Tansy, who was eavesdropping on the conversation.

'I just chose journalism because if I win, I want to spend a day on a national newspaper,' Andy explained.

'So you knew what the essays were for!' exclaimed Tansy, impressed. Andy was a lot more perceptive than she had realized.

'It was obvious,' said Andy. He dropped his voice so that Trig and Cleo couldn't hear.

'I want', he said, 'to find my mum. And if I write a big feature in a paper and put her picture in, she just might know I love her and come home.'

Tansy noticed that he was close to tears. She didn't really know what to do.

But it did make her think. She wasn't the only one with a missing parent. And she was not the only one determined to do something about it. In lots of ways Andy was worse off than she was.

Not that she wanted him to win. No way. She was definitely Going For It!

1.00 p.m. Tansy's big moment

After lunch, Tansy went to look for her mum and make sure she knew that she was not to cheer or call out or get herself noticed in any way at all.

She spotted her mum almost at once, which wasn't surprising since she was wearing a bright-orange beaded jacket, yellow palazzo pants and a black velvet hat that looked as if someone had sat on it for an extended period of time. Whenever Clarity was uptight, she reverted to the Seventies. It was not a part of her nature that Tansy found endearing.

As she hurried over to join her, she saw to her horror that she was talking to Miss Partridge. And in between them, beaming like a Cheshire cat, was Laurence Murrin.

How could he do that? thought Tansy. How come he has the nerve to sit there with the two women in his life, and expect to get away with it? Well, if she had anything to do with it, he wouldn't.

'Oh, Laurence, you are so funny!' she heard Miss

Partridge gush in her breathy voice as she drew nearer. I'll give him funny, thought Tansy angrily.

Clarity didn't look amused either. In fact, Clarity looked as if she was about to commit a punishable offence.

Tansy was about to interrupt and sort them out, when Val the producer stepped into the centre of the hall and held up her hand for quiet.

'In just a moment, Ben Bolter will be joining us for the final run through,' she said. 'Before we start recording the show Ben will ask each contestant about their ambition. It's just to get a sound check and make sure all of you know what to say. Right, let's get going.'

The teams nodded. Tansy's stomach began fluttering as she took her place with the others.

A make-up girl dusted their faces with powder, a weedy guy with a voice like an angry budgie did important-looking things with a tape measure and a piece of chalk, and the sound technician, whose dress sense was only marginally better than Laurence's, began checking dials.

Tansy listened as a girl from Bishop Agnew told how she wanted to be a deep-sea diver and a boy from Cedarwood School went on at some length about driving a team of huskies.

'Tansy Meadows from West Green Upper, please!' Val beckoned her to step in front of the camera.

'Go for it, Tansy!' A booming voice echoed

round the hall and Tansy closed her eyes in horror as she realized that Laurence was punching the air and grinning at her.

One of the Bishop Agnew girls tittered behind her and she could see Trig and Andy exchanging smirks. She thought she might as well die now and not bother with the show. Not that it mattered what Andy thought.

She was prevented from dying by Ben Bolter, who beamed at her and turned a page on his clipboard.

'And this is Tansy Meadows, whose ambition is to be a family historian – a genealogist, in fact. That's someone who traces people's family trees, for those of you not into long words.' He gave a stagey sort of laugh. 'That's an unusual ambition, Tansy. Tell us why.'

Tansy took a deep breath. She didn't have the photo of Pongo any more. She didn't have a mum who would be any help at all. And the way she was feeling right now she didn't have anything to lose.

'I think it would be a fascinating career,' she said in her clearest voice. 'But I do have a very personal reason.'

'Yes?' encouraged Ben Bolter, casting a hasty eye over his crib sheet. Tansy took a deep breath and remembered everything that she had learned about the Dramatic Pause. This was the moment when she would have raised the photograph to the camera and looked deeply moved.

'I want', she said, looking straight into the camera, 'to help people trace their ancestry. But first, more than anything, I want to find my father.'

She was aware of a gasp from some of the kids in the audience and then a muffled murmur.

'And where is your father?' asked Ben, conscious that no one had told him that this was going to happen, but aware that it might make a good publicity story for the show.

'I don't know, Ben,' she said, hoping she looked pitiful but pretty. 'I don't even know who my father is.'

1.20 p.m. Trouble in store

After that, things happened rather fast. Val the producer ordered an immediate break and went into a huddle with Ben Bolter and the film crew. The man with the tape measure and chalk flounced across the studio looking miffed and muttering about schedules and his migraine coming on. Andy, Jade and the others rushed up to Tansy and were about to starting pumping her for information when Laurence and her mother appeared, with Miss Partridge close on their heels, wearing her 'I am most displeased' expression.

Her friends melted away, sensing that what was to come was not going to be a bundle of laughs.

'Tansy,' said her mother with a catch in her voice. 'How could you? Our private business – here? In front of all these people?'

Tansy looked at the floor and then at her mother's stricken face. What had seemed a great idea a moment before suddenly seemed something of a mistake.

Miss Partridge looked pink and agitated.

'You were supposed to talk about investigating family trees,' she gabbled. 'Just as you did in your winning essay. This . . . this . . .' She waved a hand in the air. 'Well, it was very thoughtless.'

Tansy kept staring at the floor.

'How could you do that to your mother?' demanded Laurence. 'Going behind her back like that – it's despicable!'

That did it.

'You're a fine one to talk after what you've been doing!' she exploded with tears in her eyes. 'Carrying on with another woman and pretending to my mum that she's special!'

Clarity gasped. Laurence gulped. Miss Partridge stepped forward.

'Tansy, please, not here, not now . . .'

Tansy stepped back.

'Oh no, you wouldn't want me to make a fuss now, would you? Not since you *are* the other woman!'

Elinor Partridge's mouth dropped open in horror and she turned pale.

Clarity looked close to tears.

Laurence looked from Clarity to Miss Partridge and back at Tansy, who was staring at him defiantly.

'I think', he said, 'it is time you did some explaining, young lady.'

Before Tansy had a chance to open her mouth, Val the producer strode over to them, clipboard under her arm.

'We simply have to start recording the show in twenty minutes,' she said briskly. 'And our schedule is so tight that we can't possibly run the risk of any more disruptions. I think we had better substitute Jade Williams in your place, Tansy.'

Tansy looked at her in disbelief.

'But you can't ... I mean, that's not fair!' she cried. 'I haven't done anything wrong. And Jade doesn't even want to do it!' she added for good measure.

Val fixed her with a steely stare.

'I'll give you ten minutes,' she said. 'If you cannot give me a guarantee that, in the event of getting to the final, you don't mention missing fathers, then I'm afraid your place in the team is forfeit. Understand?'

Tansy nodded dumbly.

So much for her brilliant scheme. Even if her father was out there next Saturday morning, watching the show, he would never know who she was. Not now. Not ever.

1.30 p.m. Examining the evidence

'So,' said Laurence firmly, after they had all gone out into the foyer to talk, 'what is all this ridiculous nonsense about me carrying on with Miss Partridge? As if!'

Elinor Partridge glared at him.

'Not, of course,' he added hastily, 'that it wouldn't be delightful to . . .'

Clarity glared at him.

'Though, of course, I wouldn't . . . that is, couldn't . . .'

'Oh, shut up!' Tansy shouted. 'You may fool my mum but you don't fool me! You see, I've got this!'

She pulled the letter from her pocket and shoved it under Laurence's nose.

'What's this?' he said.

For the first time, Tansy's mother spoke.

'I think', she said, 'that is what we both want to know.'

1.35 p.m. Sorting things out

Tansy felt a bit stupid. Clarity looked overjoyed. Miss Partridge clucked around them and bought polystyrene cups of tea which in her excitement she spilt all over the table.

'So you see,' said Laurence, 'I must have put the first page in the envelope and mailed it to you and left the second page in the book. I gave the book to Miss Partridge on Thursday because she said she had a pupil interested in Africa.'

Tansy had one last go.

'But Mum hasn't had a letter from you,' she protested.

Clarity smiled the blissful grin of a woman reprieved.

'The post hadn't come when we left,' she said. 'It'll be waiting when we get home. Everything's just fine.'

For you, maybe, thought Tansy. It seems that not only am I destined never to find my dad but I may well get permanently lumbered with Laurence. There is no justice.

1.45 p.m. The show begins

'Are you OK?' asked Andy as Tansy took her place with the team, having promised Val the producer that she would behave like a perfect angel.

Tansy nodded.

'Don't worry,' said Andy, 'you can still find your dad. There are lots of ways of hunting people down. I'll help if you like,' he added, squeezing her hand unexpectedly.

What happened next was equally unexpected. Tansy's mouth went dry. Her heart did a sort of back flip with double pike and the skin at the back of her neck tingled.

She looked at Andy. He looked at her. And grinned.

He is, thought Tansy, very caring. And if you ignore the ears, rather cute.

Not, of course, that I fancy him.

Not at all.

*

2.00 p.m. Half-time

The show was going brilliantly. By the end of the Go for Cash rounds West Green were in the lead, but the team games were still to come. Andy and Tansy had to run back to back down the room which for some reason made Tansy's knees turn to water, but West Green fell behind. Bishop Agnew were now four points ahead.

Then just before the next round, Matthew Santer announced in a weak voice that he felt slightly ill – and proceeded to faint in a rather ungainly heap in front of the floor manager.

'Take a break!' called the guy with the tape measure, as he swallowed two painkillers and muttered about youth programmes being awfully dire for his blood pressure. 'West Green reserve, please!'

Jade turned to Scott, who was sitting behind her.

'That's you!' she said. 'Boys replace boys, girls replace girls. Good luck!'

Scott froze.

'Go on, Scott!' several of his friends urged. 'Good luck, mate!'

Scott didn't move.

Jade noticed that he was looking very pale. Maybe there was a bug going round. Perhaps that was what Matthew was suffering from.

'Are you OK?' she asked gently.

Scott glanced at her.

'I can't do it,' he whispered. 'I can't.'

'Yes you can,' urged Jade. 'Once you are up there, you'll be fine. I promise.'

The floor manager, whose face was turning a livid shade of puce, flicked his hair with the back of his hand and tutted.

'WE don't actually have all day, you know!' he simpered. 'It's too, too trying!'

'Scott,' whispered Jade. 'Go for it. You can do it. I know you can.'

He gave her a long steady look and Jade noticed that her letter was sticking out of his jeans pocket, and it was open.

He nodded slowly.

'OK,' he said. 'I'll try. Thanks.'

Jade took a deep breath and started praying.

West Green pulled back to level pegging after the brain-teaser round and everything depended on the Go For The Finish obstacle race.

Ursula put the team into an early lead, and Andy and Tansy kept up the pace. Poor Abigail got caught in the crawling net, which put them back in third place but Trig kept up a cracking place and by the time Scott was due to go, they were neck and neck with Bishop Agnew.

'Come on, Scott!' Jade yelled so loudly that her voice carried above everyone else. 'You can do it!'

Tansy didn't dare look. They had to win. They *had* to.

Scott belted round the course and reached the

finish two seconds ahead of Bishop Agnew.

They'd done it. West Green had won.

Everyone cheered, Jade loudest of all. Scott looked across into the audience and caught her eye.

And grinned from ear to ear.

Jade was so happy she wanted to cry. And very nearly did.

'And on the individual points, we have a tie,' announced Ben Bolter, grinning at the camera. 'Tansy Meadows and Andy Richards – a tie-breaker to decide.'

Tansy's heart was racing. If she got this question right before Andy did, she would win the major prize. She could ask for someone to start tracing her dad.

As Ben Bolter was explaining the rules to Camera Three, Tansy glanced at Andy. He was pale with concentration and she noticed he was digging his fingers into the palms of his hand. He looked as if his whole life depended on getting this right. He looked so nervous. He looked so cute.

She thought about Clarity. How infuriating she was, how embarrassing, how irresponsible. And how much she loved her. If her mum went missing, Tansy knew she would never be happy again.

'And the question is – fingers on buzzers, please, – *Who built St Paul's Cathedral?*'

That's easy, thought Tansy. Go on, Andy. Go on.

Andy pressed the buzzer.

'Sir Christopher Wren,' he said triumphantly.

A cheer went round the hall.

Andy had won. And to her great surprise, Tansy didn't mind at all.

'You were brilliant!' said Jade. 'We'd never have won if it hadn't been for you.'

'It was luck,' said Scott modestly. 'The others had done all the difficult bits – I'd have been useless if I'd had to talk.'

He looked at the floor and scuffed the toe of his shoe.

'Actually,' he said, 'we ought to talk.'

Jade nodded.

'Yes we should,' she said.

'And until I read your letter, I thought you hated my family,' he said. 'I never thought about it making you miss your folks.'

Jade nodded.

'It was just that round at your house, with your parents and brothers and sisters, and that aunt from Italy – well, it all came back. How we used to have tea on Saturdays while Dad watched the rugby and how Mum and I used to tease him when his team lost – and then how Gran would come round and play cards and cheat like crazy to win. And I was jealous. Horribly madly jealous.'

Scott stared at her.

'Jealous?' he asked.

Jade nodded.

'Don't you see?' she said. 'I wanted what you had. A family, noise, teasing – all that stuff. I was cross that your mum and dad were alive and nagging you about homework and mine were dead and . . .'

Her voice caught and she stopped.

'I just wanted to run away from it all,' she said. 'But not because they weren't good enough. Because it was so good. And I missed it all so much.'

Scott sighed.

'I've been a jerk, haven't I?' he said. 'Can we start over?'

Jade's eyes widened.

'You mean . . .?'

'Can we go out again?' asked Scott. 'Only if you want to.'

'Oh yes,' said Jade. 'I want to.'

'Oh good,' said Scott.

And he kissed her. In front of everyone. Even Miss Partridge. And Jade didn't mind one bit.

5 p.m. Celebration time

After the show, everyone crowded around Andy to hear about his prize. Not only did he get a whole day in London with the features editor of the *Daily Mail* but he was going to be on Mega TV's *Kids Speak Out!* show. For a moment, Tansy couldn't help feeling jealous – after all, she could have been the winner. But then Andy grinned that lopsided grin and she knew she'd done the right thing. She just hoped that she wasn't going to get too much of a blasting from her mum when they got home.

Certainly Clarity didn't look too miffed right now. She and Laurence were holding hands, which was fairly obscene given that half of Year Nine could see them. If this relationship was going to continue, Tansy would have to give her mother a few firm guidelines about her behaviour.

She was about to suggest that they went home, away from public view, when Andy came over, followed by a tall, thickset man with greying hair and red cheeks.

'My dad's taking me and my brother out for a pizza to celebrate,' he said. He pulled his ear lobe and looked around the car park as if it were the most fascinating place on earth.

'Do you want to come you don't have to,' he said in a rush.

Tansy grinned. Andy looked really endearing when he was embarrassed. If she went to supper with him, not only could she get to know him better – which she quite liked the idea of – but she'd be out of the way of any punishment her mother had planned.

'I'd love to,' she said. 'Mum!'

She beckoned her mother who thankfully released Laurence's hand and came over.

'Andy's asked me out for a pizza – is that OK?'

Clarity looked as excited as if Tansy had announced her forthcoming attendance at a

Buckingham Palace garden party.

'Wonderful, darling!' she enthused. She beamed at Andy.

'And are you two an item?' she asked.

'Mum!' hissed Tansy.

There were times when she thought her mother should carry a Government Health Warning.

'Sorry,' she muttered to Andy as they climbed into his father's car which, Tansy noted with some satisfaction was a series 5 BMW.

'That's OK,' said Andy, dropping his voice so that his small and rather muddy brother wouldn't hear. 'Can we?'

'Can we what?' asked Tansy.

'Be an item?' said Andy.

Tansy hesitated. Andy certainly wasn't a dish like Todd. But then Andy was understanding about missing parents and took time to listen. And Andy was here and Todd was nowhere.

She grinned at Andy.

'Why not?' she said.

When Tansy got home, full of pepperoni pizza and double-chocolate fudge sundae, she found her mum sitting on the settee, idly channel-hopping on the TV. Now I shall be for it, thought Tansy, hanging up her jacket and praying that her mother would not go totally ballistic.

'Have a good evening?' asked Clarity.

Tansy nodded.

127

'Where's Laurence?' asked Tansy, playing for time.

'I told him I wanted to be alone with you,' replied her mum. 'I think it's time you and I had a talk.'

She is going to kill me, thought Tansy. Maybe it would be best if I got in first.

'Look, Mum,' she began, 'I'm really sorry about this afternoon. I didn't think about all the other parents and how you would feel about them knowing.'

Clarity inclined her head.

'No, you didn't,' she agreed, 'but then I didn't think years ago about how you would feel not knowing who your father was, did I?'

She took Tansy's hand.

'Darling, I thought I was doing what was best. But perhaps I was wrong all along. You see, I haven't been totally honest.'

Tansy stared at her.

'When I knew I was going to have a baby, I really wasn't sure whether Jordan or Pongo was the father. I know, I know,' she said as Tansy tried to interrupt, 'it was irresponsible and dangerous – I've regretted it all my life. But that is how it was.'

Tansy nodded slowly.

'As soon as you were born, it was obvious. Those wonderful eyes, the heart-shaped face, everything was just like Pongo. I knew Pongo had gone back to America to get married but I was clutching at straws, and I wrote to him.'

Tansy gasped.

'You said you didn't have an address,' she accused.

'I lied,' her mother admitted. 'I was trying to protect you – I didn't want you to know that he never wrote back.'

'Never?' whispered Tansy.

Clarity shook her head.

'I wrote five times in all, and I even sent a photograph. He never replied. Not once.'

Tansy's shoulders sagged.

Somewhere in the world she had a father. The father she had dreamed about, the one who would take her out and make a fuss of her and be over the moon to have found her. Now she knew that dream would never come true.

My own father doesn't care, she thought. I don't matter at all.

'Why didn't you tell me all this ages ago?' she asked, trying not to cry.

Clarity sighed.

'I always thought it would hurt you too much – knowing that your father just didn't want to know. And as time went on, I figured that he would have a family of his own and that even if I did find him it would just mess up a whole lot of lives. I guess it seemed easier to let you blame me, because I was around for you and could prove I loved you. I'm sorry. Really I am.'

Tansy chewed her knuckle.

'You could have flown out to Illinois and confronted him,' suggested Tansy.

Clarity laughed.

'A single mum with a tiny baby – hardly feasible, sweetheart!' she said. 'Besides, I got to thinking that if he didn't even care enough to reply to my letters, then he wasn't good enough for my daughter. I decided to try to be a mum and a dad rolled into one. I'm sorry I didn't make a very good job of it.'

Tansy leaned over and gave her mother a bear-like hug.

'You did! You did!' she cried. 'You're the best mum in the world!'

Clarity slipped her hand in her pocket.

'This', she said 'is for you.'

She handed Tansy a picture. It was of Pongo. Not as clear or as large as the one that got washed, but Pongo nevertheless.

'Keep it,' said Clarity as Tansy tried to hand it back. 'Whatever he did and wherever he is now, he is your father after all. And I did love him.'

Tansy nodded.

'Thanks, Mum,' she said. 'But you keep it. I don't need it now. After all, I've got you.'

SUNDAY

Tansy and her mum were enjoying a Sunday morning slob around in their dressing gowns, when the front door opened and Laurence walked in. This, thought Tansy, was getting seriously worrying. Giving the guy his own key was only one step short of him moving in. He might not be quite as bad as she had thought but she certainly wasn't having him living here.

'Morning!' he said brightly, hugging Tansy's mum and planting a kiss on her forehead. 'Did you get the letter?'

Clarity nodded happily and pulled a sheet of notepaper from her handbag.

'Page one of two,' she laughed. 'So it was all a big misunderstanding. I'll go and make us all some coffee.'

After she had gone through to the kitchen,

Laurence looked at Tansy. Here comes the lecture, she thought. Let's get it over and done with.

'Has your mum told you?' he asked.

Oh great, thought Tansy. She's even discussed my parentage with him.

'Yes, as it happens,' she said curtly.

'Great!' said Laurence. 'So which have you chosen?'

Tansy frowned. What was the guy on about?

'The skiing holiday, silly,' said Laurence. 'Do you fancy France or Switzerland?'

Tansy's mouth dropped open in amazement.

'Me? Are you going to take me too?'

Clarity, coming back with a tray of coffee and biscuits, laughed.

'Of course,' she said. 'You don't think we'd leave you behind, do you?'

Laurence nudged Tansy's mum playfully, almost making her spill the coffee.

'Of course, she probably couldn't bear to put up with my company for a week,' he said.

True, thought Tansy. And then thought about mountains and skiing. And apres-ski. And dishy bronzed instructors.

'Oh, I don't know,' she said hastily. 'I think I could hack it.'

2.30 p.m. News from Holly
Tansy was supposedly doing her Biology home-work, but actually drawing red biro hearts and

writing 'Andy' all over them, and wondering how it was he kept creeping into her mind, when the doorbell rang.

'Get that, sweetheart,' called her mother, who for reasons best known to herself was lying on the bedroom floor, listening to a *Sounds of the Ocean* tape with a mud pack on her cheeks and two cucumber slices over her eyes.

Holly was on the doorstep, with her baby nephew William in a pushchair. She was wearing new black hipsters, a floral cardigan and pink vest top and looked stunning.

'Don't ask,' she said hastily. 'It was taking William out or doing mum's ironing.'

'No contest,' agreed Tansy. 'But what's with the glamour bit?'

Holly grinned.

'That's what I have to tell you – it's unbelievable!' She jigged up and down and little William shook in his pushchair.

'What's happened?' asked Tansy.

'It's this guy,' began Holly.

'Oh,' said Tansy with a grin. 'I should have guessed.'

2.45 p.m. On a mission

'You have to push William,' ordered Holly, thrusting the pushchair at Tansy and flicking her hair over her shoulder, as they walked down the road.

'Why me?'

'Because', said Holly, 'he might see me and I want to look cool.'

'Who might see you?' asked Tansy patiently.

Holly sighed ecstatically.

'This guy Paul – from the new house. He was at *GFI!* yesterday and he is so gorgeous!'

For the next five minutes, Holly talked non-stop – about Paul's eyes, Paul's deep voice, Paul's muscles and the combined effect of these attributes on Holly's heart.

'I have to see him again,' she said.

'He lives right behind your house, silly – of course you'll see him,' said Tansy reasonably.

'I have to see him *alone*,' persisted Holly. 'So this is what you have to do.'

'Hang on,' said Tansy. 'What *I* have to do?'

Holly nodded.

'He told me he plays tennis every Sunday afternoon in Beckets Park,' she said. 'That's where we're going.'

'I rather thought it might be,' said Tansy. 'But where do I come in?'

'You', said Holly, 'are going to faint.'

Tansy couldn't stop laughing. Holly was crazy. When Tansy said that no way would Paul rush to the aid of a fainting West Green kid, Holly suggested Tansy should scream and pretend to have been bitten by a snake.

When Tansy pointed out that Beckets Park was

not known for its adders, Holly thought that maybe they should let William loose on the tennis court and then retrieve him.

'He'd notice me then,' she said.

Tansy shook her head.

'Holly,' she said patiently, 'just shut up.'

Holly looked mortified.

'I think', said Tansy, 'you had better leave it to me.'

The two girls walked over to the courts.

'That's him!' hissed Holly. 'Over there! Don't look!'

Tansy sighed.

'If I don't look, I can't see him, can I?' She followed Holly's gaze to where a tall, athletically built guy was standing at the kiosk buying a drink.

'Stay there,' she said, and pushing William, she marched over to Paul.

'Are you Paul?' said Tansy firmly. The guy looked up in surprise and nodded.

'Oh good,' said Tansy, 'because my friend Holly met you yesterday at *GFI!* and she's dying to talk to you and if you don't get over there, I shall have to endure another ten minutes of hearing how great you are!'

3.15 p.m. *Walking home*

'I am definitely in love!' declared Holly. 'I mean, really, properly, this time. I think Scott was just a childish infatuation.'

Tansy said nothing.

'Did you hear him say he'll phone me?'

Tansy nodded.

'Do you think he will?'

Tansy nodded again.

'When? What should I say? Should I be really cool or what? Do you think he'll ask me to go out?'

Tansy shook her head.

'I doubt it,' she said.

Holly looked horror-struck.

'Why not?' she asked.

'Because he's unlikely to get a word in edgeways,' grinned Tansy.

Holly pulled a face.

'You just don't understand what it's like to be truly, madly, deeply in love,' she said.

'Yes I do,' said Tansy.

'You do? Who?' Holly gabbled.

Tansy paused.

'Andy,' she said.

Holly looked gobsmacked.

'But he's not your type at all!' she protested. 'You said your dream guy had to be tall and clever and rich and –'

'I know,' said Tansy. 'But on second thoughts, dreams can be disappointing. Andy's really cute. And understanding. And what's more he's here. Now. And that's what counts.'

Want to find out
what happens to
the girls in
another great
What a Week story?

Then sneak a peek
over the page ...

Jade thumped her fist on the table, sending peas spinning over the tablecloth.

'I don't believe you! You said Allegra could go out this Wednesday – I heard you!'

'Allegra is a year older than you and besides, she's going to the theatre. It's different.'

Jade pushed back her chair and leapt to her feet.

'Oh, well, it would be, wouldn't it?' she stormed. 'You make quite sure everything's different for your kids. I'm just the hanger-on, aren't I? You don't –'

'JADE! David, say something.'

David glaced up from the evening paper he had been reading.

'Apologize to your aunt, Jade,' he said mildly and returned to the financial pages.

'What for? Wanting a life? I'd have thought you'd be pleased I was going out. After all, you don't like me being here, do you?'

Paula was opening her mouth to reply when the front door bell rang.

'I'll get it – then you can all sit and talk about me behind my back!'

Jade stormed out of the kitchen, slamming the door behind her. I mustn't cry, she told herself firmly. I won't give them the satisfaction.

From *What a Week to Break Free* – available now!

What a Week
to Break
Free

by Rosie Rushton

The school activity weekend is coming up and everyone's got big plans – which don't include the organized activities. Canoeing, abseiling and mountain biking are all very well but there are more important things to consider – like boys ...

Poor Jade, however, is in serious trouble. She desperately needs to get away from her so-called 'home' and start a new life. But can she carry off her plans?

What a Week

to Fall in Love

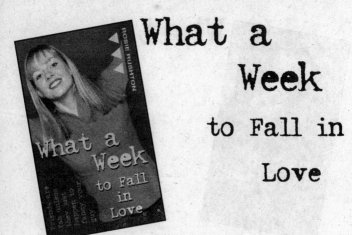

by Rosie Rushton

Holly's having a *proper* party for her fourteenth birthday – a party that her parents aren't invited to, but boys *definitely* are. Especially Scott, Holly's ex, who she intends to get back from the claws of Ella.

But when her mum cancels the party, Holly devises an extremely clever plan. Unfortunately, clever plans have a way of backfiring, especially where parents are concerned . . .